ALSO BY ALICE HOFFMAN

The Probable Future

Blue Diary

The River King

Local Girls

Here on Earth

Practical Magic

Second Nature

Turtle Moon

Seventh Heaven

At Risk

Illumination Night

Fortune's Daughter

White Horses

Angel Landing

The Drowning Season

Property Of

FOR CHILDREN

Green Angel

Indigo

Aquamarine

Horsefly

Fireflies

# BLACKBIRD HOUSE

Alice Hoffman

# BLACKBIRD
# HOUSE

DOUBLEDAY

New York   London   Toronto
Sydney   Auckland

PUBLISHED BY DOUBLEDAY
a division of Random House, Inc.,

DOUBLEDAY and the portrayal of an anchor
with a dolphin are registered trademarks of
Random House, Inc.

Excerpts from this work first appeared in the *Boston
Globe Magazine, Boulevard, Five Points, Harvard Review,
Hunger Mountain, The Kenyon Review, The Missouri Review,
Prairie Schooner*, and *Southwest Review.*

*Book design by Marysarah Quinn*

Library of Congress Cataloging-in-Publication Data
Hoffman, Alice.
Blackbird House / Alice Hoffman — 1st ed.
p.   cm.
1. Women—Massachusetts—Fiction. 2. Home
ownership—Fiction. 3. Massachusetts—Fiction.
4. Dwellings—Fiction. I. Title.
PS3558.O3447B55   2004
813´.54—dc22
2004007958

ISBN 0-385-50761-5
PRINTED IN THE UNITED STATES OF AMERICA
September 2004
FIRST EDITION
1 3 5 7 9 10 8 6 4 2

# CONTENTS

# ACKNOWLEDGMENTS

The author wishes to thank the editors of the magazines in which some of these stories first appeared: the *Boston Globe Magazine, Boulevard, Five Points, Harvard Review, Hunger Mountain, The Kenyon Review, The Missouri Review, Prairie Schooner, Southwest Review*. Special gratitude to Richard Bausch for his kindness and generosity.

Thank you to the women willing to run off to sea: Perri Klass, Alexandra Marshall, and especially Jill McCorkle. Thanks to my first readers: Maggie Stern Terris, Elizabeth Hodges, Carol DeKnight, Sue Standing, and Tom Martin. Gratitude to Elaine Markson and to Gary Johnson. To my sons, thank you for helping me to understand. And many thanks to Q. who showed me what courage looked like.

# BLACKBIRD HOUSE

# THE EDGE OF THE WORLD

## I.

*I*T WAS SAID THAT BOYS SHOULD GO ON
their first sea voyage at the age of ten, but
surely this notion was never put forth by
anyone's mother. If the bay were to be raised
one degree in temperature for every woman
who had lost the man or child she loved at
sea, the water would have boiled, throwing
off steam even in the dead of winter, poach-
ing the bluefish and herrings as they swam.

Every May, the women in town gathered
at the wharf. No matter how beautiful the
day, scented with new grass or spring onions,
they found themselves wishing for snow and
ice, for gray November, for December's

gales and land-locked harbors, for fleets that returned, safe and sound, all hands accounted for, all boys grown into men. Women who had never left Massachusetts dreamed of the Middle Banks and the Great Banks the way some men dreamed of hell: The place that could give you everything you might need and desire. The place that could take it all away.

This year the fear of what might be was worse than ever, never mind gales and storms and starvation and accidents, never mind rum and arguments and empty nets. This year the British had placed an embargo on the ships of the Cape. No one could go in or out of the harbor, except unlawfully, which is what the fishermen in town planned to do come May, setting off on moonless nights, a few sloops at a time, with the full knowledge that every man caught would be put to death for treason and every boy would be sent to Dartmoor Prison in England—as good as death, people in town agreed, but colder and some said more miserable.

Most people made their intentions known right away, those who would go and those who would stay behind to man the fort beside Long Pond if need be, a battle station that was more of a cabin than anything, but at least it was something solid to lean against should a man have to take aim and fire. John Hadley was among those who wanted to stay. He made that clear, and everyone knew he had his reasons. He had just finished the little house in the hollow that he'd been working on with his older son, Vincent, for nearly three years. During this time, John Hadley and Vincent had gone out fishing each summer, searching out bluefish and halibut, fish large enough so that you could fill up your catch in a very short time. John's sloop was small, his desires were few: he wanted to give his wife this house, nothing fancy, but carefully made all the same, along with the acreage around it, a meadow filled with wild grapes and winterberry. Wood for building was hard to come by, so John had used old wrecked boats for the joists, deadwood he'd found in the shipyard, and when there was none of that to be had, he used fruitwood he'd culled from his property, though people insisted applewood and pear wouldn't last. There was no glass in the windows, only oiled paper, but the light that came through was dazzling and yellow; little flies buzzed in and out of the light, and everything seemed slow, molasses slow, lovesick slow.

John Hadley felt a deep love for his wife, Coral, more so than anyone might guess. He was still tongue-tied in her presence, and he had the foolish notion that he could give her something no other man could. Something precious and lasting and hers alone. It was the house he had in mind whenever he looked at Coral. This was what love was to him: when he was at sea he could hardly sleep without the feel of her beside him. She was his anchor, she was his home; she was the road that led to everything that mattered to John Hadley.

Otis West and his cousin Harris Maguire had helped with the plans for the house—a keeping room, an attic for the boys, a separate chamber for John and Coral. These men were good neighbors, and they'd helped again when the joists were ready, even though they both thought John was a fool for giving up the sea. A man didn't give up who he was, just to settle down. He didn't trade his freedom for turnips. Still, these neighbors spent day after day working alongside John and Vincent, bringing their oxen to help lift the crossbeams, hollering for joy when the heart of the work was done, ready to get out the good rum. The town was like that: for or against you, people helped each other out. Even old Margaret Swift, who was foolish enough to have raised the British flag on the pole outside her house, was politely served when she came into the livery store, though there were folks in town who believed that by rights she should be drinking tar and spitting feathers.

John's son Vincent was a big help in the building of the house, just as he was out at sea, and because of this they would soon be able to move out of the rooms they let at Hannah Crosby's house. But Isaac, the younger boy, who had just turned ten, was not quite so helpful. He meant to be, but he was still a child, and he'd recently found a baby blackbird that kept him busy. Too busy for other chores, it seemed. First, he'd had to feed the motherless creature every hour with crushed worms and johnnycake crumbs, then he'd had to drip water into the bird's beak from the tip of his finger. He'd started to hum to the blackbird, as if it were a real baby. He'd started to talk to it when he thought no one could overhear.

"Wild creatures belong in the wild," Coral Hadley told her son. All the same, she had difficulty denying Isaac anything. Why, she let the boy smuggle his pet into the rooms they let at the Crosbys' boarding house, where he kept the blackbird in a wooden box beside his bed.

The real joy of the house they were building, as much for John as for anyone, was that it was, indeed, a farm. They would have cows and horses to consider, rather than halibut and bluefish; predictable beasts at long last, and a large and glorious and predictable meadow as well. Rather than the cruel ocean, there would be fences, and a barn, and a deep cistern of cold well water, the only water John's boys would need or know, save for the pond at the rear of the property, where damselflies glided above the mallows in spring. John Hadley had begun to talk about milk cows and crops. He'd become fascinated with turnips, how hardy they were, how easy to grow, even in sandy soil. In town, people laughed at him. John Hadley knew this, and he didn't care. He'd traveled far enough in his lifetime. Once, he'd been gone to the island of Nevis all summer long with the Crosbys on their sloop; he'd brought Coral back an emerald, he'd thought then that was what she wanted most in the world. But she'd told him to sell it and buy land. She knew that was what he wanted.

Coral was a good woman, and John was a handsome man, tall, with dark hair and darker eyes, a Cornishman, as tough as men from Cornwall always were. All the same, he didn't have too much pride to herd sheep, or clean out a stable, or plant corn and turnips, though it meant a long-term battle with brambles and nettle. Still, his was a town of fishermen; much as soldiers who can never leave their country once they've buried their own in the earth, so here it was the North Atlantic that called to them, a graveyard for sure, but home just as certainly. And John was still one of them, at least for the present time. If a man in these parts needed to earn enough to buy fences and cows and turnips, he knew where he had to go. It would only be from May to July, John figured, and that would be the end of it, especially if he was helped by his two strong sons.

They moved into the house in April, a pale calm day when the buds on the lilacs their neighbors had planted as a welcome were just about to unfold. The house was finished enough to sleep in; there was a fireplace where Coral could cook, and the rest would come eventually. Quite suddenly, John and Coral felt as though time was unlimited, that it was among the things that would never be in short supply.

"That's where the horses will be," John Hadley told Coral. They were looking out over the field that belonged to them, thanks to those years John had spent at sea and the emerald they'd sold. "I'll name one Charger. I had a horse called that when I was young."

Coral laughed to think of him young. She saw her boys headed for the pond. The blackbird chick rode on Isaac's shoulder and flapped his wings. It was their first day, the beginning of everything. Their belongings were still in crates.

"I'll just take him with me and Vincent this one time," John said. "I promise. Then we'll concentrate on turnips."

"No," Coral said. She wanted three milk cows and four sheep and her children safe in their own beds. She thought about her youngest, mashing worms into paste for his fledgling. "Isaac can't go."

By then the brothers had reached the shores of the little pond. The frogs jumped away as they approached. The blackbird, frightened by the splashing, hopped into the safety of Isaac's shirt, and sent out a small muffled cry.

"He's like a hen," the older brother jeered. At fifteen, Vincent had grown to his full height, six foot, taller than his father; he was full of himself and how much he knew. He'd been to sea twice, after all, and he figured he was as good as any man; he already had calluses on his hands. He didn't need to go to school anymore, which was just as well, since he'd never been fond of his lessons. "He doesn't even know he can fly," he said of his brother's foundling.

"I'll teach him." Isaac felt in his shirt for the blackbird.

The feathers reminded him of water, soft and cool. Some-times Isaac let the chick sleep right beside him, on the quilt his mother had sewn out of indigo homespun.

"Nah, you won't. He's a big baby. Just like you are. He'll be walking around on your shoulder for the rest of his life."

After that, Isaac brought the blackbird into the woods every day, just to prove Vincent wrong. He climbed into one of the tall oaks and let his legs dangle over a high limb. He urged the blackbird to fly away, but the bird was now his pet, too attached to ever leave; the poor thing merely paced on his shoulder and squawked. Isaac decided to name his pet Ink. Ink was an indoor bird, afraid of the wind, and of others of his own kind. He hopped around the parlor, and nested beneath the woodstove, where it was so hot he singed his feathers. He sat on the table and sipped water from a saucer while Isaac did his studies. It was a navigation book Isaac was studying. *The Practical Navigator.* If he was not as strong as Vincent, or as experienced, then at least he could memorize the chart of the stars; he could know the latitude of where they were going and where they'd been.

"Do you think I could teach him to talk?" Isaac said dreamily to his mother one day. Ink was perched on the tabletop, making a nuisance of himself.

"What would a blackbird have to say?" Coral laughed.

"He'd say: *I'll never leave you. I'll be with you for all time.*"

Hearing those words, Coral felt faint; she said she needed some air. She went into the yard and faced the meadow and gazed at the way the tall grass moved in the wind. That night she said to her husband again, "Don't take him with you, John."

April was ending, with sheets of rain and the sound of the peepers calling from the shore of the pond. Classes would end in a few days, too—they called it a fisherman's school, so that boys were free to be sent out to work with their fathers or uncles or neighbors from May till October. The Hadleys left in the first week of that mild month, a night when there was no moon. The fog had come in; so much the better when it came to sneaking away. The British had lookouts to the east and the west, and it was best to take a northerly route. They brought along molasses, the fishing nets, johnnycake, and salted pork, and, unknown to John and Vincent, Isaac took along his blackbird as well, tucked into his jacket. As they rounded the turn out of their own harbor, Isaac took his pet from his hiding place.

"You could do it now if you wanted to," he said to the bird. "You could fly away."

But the blackbird shivered in the wind, startled, it seemed, by the sound of water. He scrambled back to the safety of Isaac's jacket, feathers puffed up, the way they always were when he was frightened.

"I told you he'd never fly." Vincent had spied the black-bird. He nudged his brother so that Isaac would help check the nets. "He's pathetic, really."

"No, he's not!"

By now they were past the fog that always clung to shore at this time of year, and the night was clear. There were so many stars in the sky, and the vast expanse of dark and light was frightening. The water was rougher than Isaac had ever seen it in their bay, and they were still not even halfway to the Middle Banks. The sloop seemed small out here, far too breakable.

"Is this the way it always is?" Isaac asked his brother. He felt sick to his stomach; there was a lurching in his bones and blood. He thought about the oak tree and the meadow and the frogs and the way his mother looked at him when he came in through the door.

"It's the way it is tonight," Vincent said.

Used to the sea, Vincent fell asleep easily, but Isaac couldn't close his eyes. John Hadley understood; he came to sit beside the boy. It was so dark that every star in the sky hung suspended above the mast, as though only inches above them. Isaac recognized the big square of Pegasus that he'd seen in his book. The night looked like spilled milk, and John Hadley pointed out Leo, the harbinger of spring, then the North Star, constant as always. John could hear the chattering of the blackbird in his son's waistcoat. He could taste his wife's farewell kiss.

"What happens if a storm comes up?" Isaac said, free to be frightened now that his brother was asleep, free to be the boy he still was. "What happens if I'm thrown overboard? Or if a whale comes along? What happens then?"

"Then I'll save you." When the wind changed John Hadley smelled turnips, he really did, and he laughed at the scent of it, how it had followed him all this way to the Middle Banks, to remind him of everything he had to lose.

## II.

SO MANY MEN WERE TAKEN IN THE MAY gale that the Methodist church on Main Street could not hold the relatives of the lost all on one day. There was a full week of services, and not a single one had a body to behold. The law suggested three months pass by before any action was taken; time after time, it was true, sailors who had been thrown off course by the cruel circumstances of the seas, then assumed drowned, had appeared at their own funerals. Once a drowned man arrived on the steps of the church, those who mourned him demanded to know where on earth he'd been all this time. Was there another woman in the West Indies or up in Nova Scotia? Had every cent he'd earned at sea been spent on rum? The truth was usually far simpler: it took a long time to get back home, out here to the edge of the world.

After the May gale the town waited an unheard-of six months before the services commenced, and even then Coral Hadley refused to have her husband and sons counted among those who were mourned. She didn't answer the door when the parson came to call; she didn't attend a single one of the services, though they were held for the husbands and sons of her friends, Harris Maguire and Otis West among them. Coral had known something would happen the morning they'd left. That was the worst part of it: she kept going back to that day, wondering what might have been if only she'd insisted on having her way. She'd found four blue eggs out on the hillock by the pond, and every egg had a hole in it. Coral had rattled each one. Nothing inside. A bad sign to find such things, a terrible sign, an omen of misfortune and of lives unfinished; futures cracked open into a powdery dust. Later that night, when the wind came up, she heard her name called aloud. When she told people about this, no one believed her, but Coral didn't care. She had gone to stand outside on the night they disappeared; though it was foggy, she went into the field where they would keep their cows, where the horse they planned to name Charger would graze, and she heard someone say, *I'll never leave you.*

As soon as news of the gale came in, she refused to mourn with the other women. Right away, she said there'd be no service, no matter what the parson advised, and all these months later she could not be moved. The tragedy of her lost family was still unproven; there were no bodies found, not even a single splinter of wood from their sloop. The women in town tried to convince Coral to let the dead be put to rest; they'd seen women in a mourning delirium before, unable to tell what was real and what was not. Even old Hannah Crosby came down the lane and told Coral she had to face up to the terrible thing that had happened. If the British had caught her men, they surely would have heard by now; John would have been taken to trial in Boston, just like the Henry brothers and so many others. There would have been some news of the boys.

"I can wait," Coral said. That and nothing more.

She had planted the field, the way she thought John would want her to. Though the ground was cold, she dug in row after row of turnips, then she planted corn; at last she sprinkled the seedpods of pink sweet peas, feed for the cows they would someday have, and for remembrance as well. John had favored sweet peas, and had brought her armfuls of the flowers when he was courting her. Her mother had said they were weeds, but, as was often the case, her mother was wrong.

Coral worked with a pick in the hot sun all summer long

and into autumn, unafraid of dirt or hard work, dressed in black, refusing to eat anything her neighbors might bring. In honor of her family, and what they must be suffering, she ate only johnnycakes and catfish caught from the pond, simmering in an old pan over the woodstove. She kept in mind those men who had reappeared at their own funerals: Robert Servich and Nathaniel Hawkes, for instance, both of them lost for months in the Indies, and now living right down the lane. She thought about turnip stew and turnip cakes and how pleased John would be when he tasted the fruit of her labors. How he'd be surprised to hear there were green onions growing wild in the far field, that there was a grapevine so huge it would keep them in jellies and jams and pies all year long.

And then, the next spring, when May arrived and the leaves were budding in shades of yellow and green, Coral realized that the blackbird had returned. It was some time before she recognized it, because the bird had turned entirely white. It sat in a branch of the big oak, where it could have easily been mistaken for a wisp of a cloud. It looked like something Coral could blink away, but it wouldn't disappear. First the bird was on her roof, then it was at her window, and then, one morning, the white blackbird tapped at the door, and that was how she knew they were gone.

In an instant she knew everything she had hoped for

was impossible. She cut off all her hair, and she tore the clothes she wore with a carving knife. She threw away her frying pan and her kettle, her spices and her liberty tea, all tossed into the pond. She might have starved to death if Hannah Crosby hadn't seen that bird circling over the property, like a vulture or a ghost. The doctor was called in; some sassafras tea and bed rest were recommended. Hannah, to her credit, suggested that Coral come back and live in the lodging rooms the family had occupied before John built the house. But she could tell, with one harsh look from Coral, the answer was no.

In another town, a widow's vandu might be suggested, and a year of Coral's labor put up for auction so that she could met her expenses, but this was not the sort of place where people were sold to the highest bidder. The Hawkes family brought over an old cow that was still a good milker, and Hannah Crosby was happy to oversee the garden to ensure there'd be a decent crop of turnips, if nothing else.

By the end of the summer, Coral Hadley was selling her turnips by the side of the road, set out in crates, trusting folks' honesty. The turnips were particularly large; one alone could last a week. People said they were so sweet, a single bite could bring a man to tears. Buyers tended to leave more money in the cash box than they needed to. Even the British soldiers took three boxes of turnips along with them for their voyage home, and they left Coral

Hadley eight shillings per box, far more than they were worth.

Seven years after the May gale, the white blackbird could still be spied. It was said Coral Hadley had tried to chase it off; she'd fired a musket at it, she'd thrown a bucket of ashes in its direction, but it wouldn't go away. Even after all these years, people remembered her suffering. Perhaps her neighbors thought it was luck to help the luckless: some of the men put up a fence around Coral's garden, and another around the barn. One spring a pair of sheep was left in her field. Another May, a dusty-gray horse that looked very much like one that belonged the Maguire family was tied up to the post outside the house. People took to leaving out food for the crow as well, crumb cakes and molasses bread, for such gifts were said to be good luck. Hannah Crosby, who so feared birds, left morsels on a stump in the center of the meadow and swore the blackbird had once eaten from the palm of her hand.

One summer day, Coral Hadley went out early to feed the sheep, and the cow, and the horse she had named Charger, and there was a man in her yard. Each spring she had planted sweet peas; now they were everywhere, knee high, blossoming, purple and white and pink. Coral knew she wasn't the person she used to be: her teeth were falling out, ground down by nightmares; her hair had turned white. People in town said she was hurrying her old age, rushing forward to meet her husband, John, and her children in the hereafter, but really she was rushing toward this moment, this instant, this very breath.

## III.

THE MAY GALE HAD SURPRISED THEM, AS IT HAD surprised everyone else who was fishing in the Middle Banks. One moment there'd been a sea of glass, the next a sea of mountains. They did the best any crew might have done; even Isaac managed as well as could be expected as they tried to drive leeward. But in the force of the storm, the sloop broke apart, and there was nothing anyone could have done. It happened not slowly, but all at once, as though a giant had picked them up and crushed them with a single stroke. Everything splintered; everything broke; everything was devoured by the sea. Things that couldn't be were. Things that should never have happened were there before their eyes. Vincent knew how bad it was when his brother threw the blackbird into the sky, threw him with both hands, a last desperate act of love.

John Hadley's last act was to roll the molasses barrel to Vincent so he could float with it. John then grabbed his younger son around his chest, and he and Isaac disappeared almost at once. To his great shame, Vincent clung to the barrel. That was how the British schooner found him; they'd had to pry his frozen fingers from the metal band around the center of the wood. Though they were the enemy, and had no choice but to take him to Dartmoor Prison, the soldiers congratulated him on his fortitude. They did not ask if he'd been at sea all alone, and he did not tell them that he had watched his father and his brother drown. If that was fortitude, it was something he didn't care to possess. If that was strength, he wanted none of it. He wished he'd let go of that barrel that had saved him.

Vincent Hadley was in prison in England for five years, until the war was over, and then he was released without a shilling. Prison had been a strange dream of hearing other men talk and rant and list their regrets. As for Vincent, he never said much, although it was evident he had regrets as well. He cried for the first year, pathetically, horribly, salt-water tears, and then he stopped. By the time he was released, he probably could not have cried if he'd been stabbed through the chest. There was no water left inside him. There was nothing inside him at all.

He got the only sort of work he felt capable of doing, signing on to one ship after another, always checking for a route that might bring him closer to home. Another man might have carried with him a justified fear of the sea; he might have lived in dread of storms a man couldn't fight, of gales that came up suddenly at the hour when the sea seemed calm as glass. But in fact, Vincent was fearless. If there was something dangerous to be done, he need simply be asked, not even commanded. He would dive into the coldest tide and scrape barnacles from beneath a sloop. He would retrieve anchors from the deep. He would wrestle with bluefish, and he had the marks of their teeth on his arms to show that, although he'd won many fights, the battles had been fierce.

At last he got to Virginia. He was a man of twenty-seven by then, and he still didn't talk much. He had no answers, and he wanted no questions. He'd spent so much time in the West Indies that his blood had thinned; he was no longer used to the cold, and he knew as he traveled it would get colder still. The first thing he did after arriving in Virginia was buy a deerskin jacket. The second was to start to edge his way north, always fishing, always taking on the most dangerous work. Whenever the men he worked alongside said go back, whenever the sea was at its worst, Vincent said go forward. He considered writing a letter home, explaining where he'd been, but he'd never been much for writing, and when it came down to it, what did he have to say? That the blackbird had dipped its wings into the cold, roiling sea, where it was covered in foam? That he'd guessed it would drown, but instead it had suddenly flown upward, that pet of his brother's that had never before taken flight. It had disappeared into a cloud.

It took him twelve years to think of what he would say.

He was a tall, handsome, quiet man; he took after his father in some ways. Women fell in love with him, but he wasn't concerned with such things. He still had the mark of the copper band from that barrel he'd clung to so desperately embedded in the fingers on both hands. Some people said the marks looked like rings, and perhaps that's what they were. He was wedded to something already, and no woman in Virginia or Maryland or New York could tie him to her for longer than a few days.

It was summer when he reached the Cape. He started down the King's Highway, that rutted sandy lane that would take him home. When he stopped at taverns, and heard Massachusetts voices, he felt as though he'd been gone far longer than twelve years. He wanted to walk and get the feel of the place. He wanted to take his time and see milkweed, and wild blueberries, and cranberry bogs. He'd been at sea for so long, and was so accustomed to its constant motion, it was a while before he got used to solid ground. He slept beneath the oak trees and ordered bread and gravy and little else in the taverns where he occasionally stopped. He had taught himself not to long for water or hunger for food. There wasn't much he was attached to in this world. The bite marks on his arms from the bluefish burned, but he paid the scars no mind. He thought about how sure he'd been of himself, once; how he'd believed he was as knowledgeable as any man. He thought about the damselflies gliding over the pond, and the sound of the frogs plashing in the water, and the yellow light coming in through the windows of the house his father built. He thought about how love could move you in ways you wouldn't have imagined, one foot in front of the other, even when you thought you had nothing left inside. He smelled lilacs after a while, and the scent of wild onions. There were the sweet peas, right in front of him, already in bloom, acres of them, grown carefully from seed, a pink-hued and endless sea.

# THE WITCH OF TRURO

WITCHES TAKE THEIR NAMES FROM PLACES, for places are what give them their strength. The place need not be beautiful, or habitable, or even green. Sand and salt, so much the better. Scrub pine, plumberry, and brambles, better still. From every bitter thing, after all, something hardy will surely grow. From every difficulty, the seed that's sewn is that much stronger. Ruin is the milk all witches must drink; it's the lesson they learn and the diet they're fed upon. Ruth Declan lived on a bluff that was called Blackbird's Hill, and so she was called Ruth Blackbird Hill, a fitting name, as her hair

was black and she was so light-footed she could disappear
right past a man and he wouldn't see anything, he'd just feel
a rush of wind and pick up the scent of something remi-
niscent of orchards and the faint green odor of milk.

Ruth kept cows, half a dozen, but they gave so much
into their buckets she might have had twenty. She took her
cows for walks, as though they were pets, along the sand-
rutted King's Highway, down to the bay, where they grazed
on marsh grass. Ruth Blackbird Hill called her cows her
babies and hugged them to her breast; she patted their
heads and fed them sugar from the palm of her hand, and
that may have been why their milk was so sweet. People
said Ruth Blackbird Hill sang to her cows at night, and that
whoever bought milk from her would surely be bewitched.
Not that anyone believed in such things anymore. All the
same, when Ruth came into town, the old women tied bits
of hemp into witchknots on their sleeves for protection.
The old men looked to see if she was wearing red shoes,
always the mark of a witch. Ruth avoided these people; she
didn't care what they thought. She would have happily
stayed on Blackbird Hill and never come down, but two
things happened: First came smallpox, which took her father and her mother, no matter how much sassafras tea
they were given, and how tenderly Ruth cared for them.
Then came the fire, which took the house and the land.

On the night of the fire, Ruth Blackbird Hill stood in

the grass and screamed. People could hear her all the way in Eastham and far out to sea. She watched the pear and the apple and the peach trees burning. She watched the grass turn red as blood. She had risked her life to save her cows, running into the smoky barn, and now they gathered round her, lowing, leaking milk, panicked. It was not enough that she should lose her mother and her father, one after the other, now she had lost Blackbird Hill, and with it she had lost herself. The fire raged for two days, until a heavy rain began to fall. People in town said that Ruth killed a toad and nailed it to a hickory tree, knowing that rain would follow, but it was too late. The hill was burned to cinders; it was indeed a blackbird's hill, black as night, black as the look in Ruth's eyes, black as the future that was assuredly hers.

Ruth sat on the hillside until her hair was completely knotted and her skin was the color of the gray sky up above. She might have stayed there forever, but after some time went by, her cows began to cry. They were weak with hunger, they were her babies still, and so Ruth took them into town. One day, people looked out their windows and a blackbird seemed to swoop by, followed by a herd of skinny milk-cows that had all turned to pitch in the fire. Ruth Blackbird Hill made herself a camp right on the beach; she slept there with no shelter, no matter the weather. The only food she ate was what she dug up in the shallows: clams and whelks. She may have drunk the green, thin milk her cows gave, though it was still tinged with cinders. She may have bewitched herself to protect herself from any more pain. Perhaps that was the reason she could sleep in the heat or the rain; why it was said she could drink salt water.

Anyone would have guessed the six cows would have bolted for someone else's farmland and a field of green grass, but they stayed where they were, on the beach, beside Ruth. People in town said you could hear them all crying at night; it got so bad the fish were frightened out of the bay, and the whelks disappeared, and the oysters buried themselves so deeply they couldn't be found.

It was May, the time of year when the men went to sea. Perhaps a different decision might have been considered if the men been home from the Great Banks and the Middle Banks, where their sights were set on mackerel and cod. Perhaps Ruth would have been run out of town. As it was, Susan Crosby and Easter West devised a plan of their own. They won Ruth Blackbird Hill over slowly, with plates of oatcakes and kettles of tea. They took their time, the way they might with a fox or a dove, any creature that was easily startled. They sat on a log of dritfwood and told Ruth that sorrow was what this world was made of, but that it was her world still. At first she would not look at them, yet they could tell she was listening. She was a young woman, a girl really, nineteen at most, although her hands looked as hard as an old woman's, with ropes of veins that announced her hardships.

Susan and Easter brought Ruth over to Lysander Wynn's farm, where he'd built a blacksmithing shed. It took half the morning to walk there, with the cows stopping to graze by the road, dawdling until Ruth coaxed them on. It was a bright-blue day, and the women from town felt giddy now that they'd made a firm decision to guide someone else's fate, what their husbands might call "interference" had they but known. As for Ruth, she still had a line of black cinders under her fingernails. There was eelgrass threaded through her hair. She had the notion that these two women, Susan and Easter, known for their good works and their kindly attitudes, were about to sell her into servitude. She simply couldn't see any other reason for them to be walking along with her, swatting the cows on the rear to speed them on, waving away the flies. The awful thing was that Ruth wasn't completely opposed to being sold. She didn't want to think. She didn't want to remember anything. She didn't even want to speak.

They reached the farm that Lysander had bought from the Hadley family. He'd purchased the property mainly because it was the one place in the area from which there was no view of the sea, for that was exactly what he wanted. The farm was only a mile from the closest shore, but it sat in a hollow, with tall oaks and scrub pine and a field of sweet peas and brambles nearby. As a younger man,

Lysander had been a sailor, he'd gone out with the neighbors to the Great Banks, and it was there he'd had his accident. A storm had come up suddenly, and the sloop had listed madly, throwing Lysander into the sea. It was so cold he had no time to think, save for a fleeting thought of Jonah, of how a man could be saved when he least expected it, in ways he could have never imagined.

He wondered if perhaps the other men on board, Joseph Hansen and Edward West, had had the foresight to throw him a side of salt pork for him to lean on, for, just when he expected to drown, something solid was suddenly beneath him. Something hard and cold as ice. Something made of scales rather than flesh or water or wood; a creature who certainly was not intent on Lysander's salvation. The fish to whose back he clung was a halibut, a huge one—two hundred, maybe three hundred pounds, Edward West later said. Lysander rode the halibut like he rode his horse, Domino, until he was bucked off. All at once his strength was renewed by his panic; he started swimming, harder than he ever had before. Lysander was almost to the boat when he felt it, the slash of the thing against him, and the water turned red right away. He was only twenty at the time, too young to have this happen. Dead or alive, either would have been better than what had befallen him. He wished he had drowned that day, because when he was hauled into the boat his neighbors had to finish the job and cut off the leg at the thigh, then cauterize the wound with gunpowder and whiskey.

Lysander had some money saved, and the other men in town contributed the rest, and the farm was bought soon after. The shed was built in a single afternoon, and the anvil brought down from Boston. Luckily, Lysander had the blacksmith's trade in his family, on his father's side, so it came naturally to him. The hotter the work was, the better he liked it. He could stick his hand into the flame fueled by the bellow and not feel a thing. But let it rain, even a fleeting drizzle, and he would start to shiver. He ignored the pond behind the house entirely, though there were catfish there that were said to be delectable. Fishing was for other men. Water was for fools. As for women, they were a dream he didn't bother with. In his estimation, the future was no farther away than the darkness of evening; it consisted of nothing more than a sprinkling of stars in the sky.

Lysander used a crutch made of applewood that bent when he leaned upon it but was surprisingly strong when need be. He had hit a prowling skunk on the head with the crutch and knocked it unconscious. He had dug through a mat of moss for a wild orchid that smelled like fire when he held it up to his face. He slept with the crutch by his side in bed, afraid to be without it. He liked to walk in the woods, and sometimes he imagined he would be better off if he just lay down between the logs and the moss and stayed there, forevermore. Then someone would need their horse shod; they would come up the road and ring the bell that hung on the wall of the shed, and Lysander would have to scramble back from the woods. But he thought about remaining where he was, hidden, unmoving; he imagined it more often than anyone might have guessed. Crows would light upon his shoulders, crickets would crawl into his pockets, fox would lie down beside him and never even notice he was there.

He was in the woods on the day they brought Ruth Blackbird Hill and her cows to the farm. Sometimes when he was very quiet Lysander thought he saw another man in the trees. He thought it might be the sailor who'd built the house, the widow Hadley's husband, who'd been lost at sea. Or perhaps it was himself, weaving in and out of the shadows, the man he might have been.

Susan Crosby and Easter West explained the situation: the parents lost, the house and meadows burned down, the way Ruth was living on the beach, unprotected, unable to support herself, even to eat. In exchange for living in Lysander's house, she would cook and clean for him. Ruth kept her back to them as they discussed her fate; she patted one of her cows, a favorite of hers she called Missy. Lysander Wynn was just as bitter as Ruth Blackbird Hill was. He was certain the women from town wouldn't have brought Ruth to the farm if he'd been a whole man, able to get up the stairs to the attic, where they suggested Ruth

sleep. He was about to say no, he was more than willing to
get back to work in the fires of his shop, when he noticed
that Ruth was wearing red boots. They were made of old
leather, mud-caked; all the same, Lysander had never seen
shoes that color, and he felt touched in some way. He
thought about the color of fire. He thought about flames.
He thought he would never be hot enough to get the chill
out of his body or the water out of his soul.

"Just as long as she never cooks fish," he heard himself
say.

Ruth Blackbird Hill laughed at that. "What makes you
think I cook at all?"

Ruth took the cows into the field of sweet peas.
Lysander's horse, Domino, rolled his eyes and ran to the
far end of the meadow, spooked. But the cows paid no attention to the gelding whatsoever, they just huddled
around Ruth Blackbird Hill and calmly began to eat wild
weeds and grass. What Lysander had agreed to didn't sink
in until Susan Crosby and Easter West left to go back to
town. *Hasn't this woman any belongings?* Lysander had called after them. *Not a thing*, they replied. *Only the cows that follow her
and the shoes on her feet.*

Well, a shoe was the one thing Lysander might have offered. He had several old boots thrown into a cabinet, useless when it came to his missing right foot. He put out
some old clothes and quilts on the stairs leading to the attic. He'd meant to finish it, turn the space into decent

rooms, but he'd had to crawl up the twisting staircase to check on the rafters, and that one attempt was enough humiliation to last him for a very long time. Anyway, the space was good enough for someone used to sleeping on the beach. When Ruth didn't come in to start supper, Lysander made himself some johnnycake, half cooked, but decent enough, along with a plate of turnips; he left a portion of what he'd fixed on the stair alongside the clothes, though he had his suspicions that Ruth might not eat. She might just starve herself sitting out in that field. She might take flight, and he'd find nothing when he woke, except for the lonely cows mooing sorrowfully.

As it turned out, Ruth was there in the morning. She'd eaten the food he'd left out for her and was already milking the cows when Lysander went out to work on a metal harness for Easter West's uncle Karl's team of mules. Those red shoes peeked out from beneath Ruth's black skirt. She was singing to the cows and they were waiting in line, patiently. The horse, Domino, had come closer, and Ruth Blackbird Hill opened her palm and gave him a lick of sugar.

In the afternoon Lysander saw her looking in the window of the shed. The fire was hot and he was sweating. He wanted to sweat out every bit of cold ocean water. He always built the fire hotter than advisable. He needed it that way. Sometimes he got a stomachache, and when he vomited, he spat out the halibut's teeth. Those teeth had gone

right through him, it seemed. He could feel them, cold, sil-
very things.

He must have looked frightening as he forged the metal
harness, covered with soot, hot as the devil, because Ruth
Blackbird Hill ran away, and she didn't come to fetch the
dinner he placed on the stair—though the food was better
than the night before, cornbread with wild onions this
time, and greens poured over with gravy. All the same, the
following morning the plate was clean and resting on the
table. Every morsel had been eaten.

Ruth Blackbird Hill didn't cook and she didn't clean,
but she kept on watching him through the window that
was made of bumpy glass. Lysander didn't look up, didn't
let on that he knew she was staring, and then, one day, she
was standing in the doorway to the shed. She was wearing
a pair of his old britches and a white shirt, but he could see
through the smoke that she had on those red shoes.

"How did you lose your leg?" Ruth asked.

He had expected nearly anything but that question. It
was rude; no one asked things like that.

"A fish bit it off," he said.

Ruth laughed and said, "No."

He could feel the heat from the iron he was working on
in his hands, his arms, his head.

"You don't believe me?" He showed her the chain he
wore around his neck, strung with halibut teeth. "I
coughed these up one by one."

"No," Ruth said again, but her voice was quieter, as though she was thinking it over. She walked right up to him, and Lysander felt something inside him quicken. He had absolutely no idea of what she might do.

Ruth Blackbird Hill put her left hand in the fire, and she would have kept it there if he hadn't grabbed her arm and pulled her back.

"See?" she said to him. Her skin felt cool, and she smelled like grass. "There are things I'm afraid of, too."

People in town forgot about Ruth; they didn't think about how she was living out at the farm any more than they remembered how she'd been camped on the beach for weeks without anyone's offering help until Susan and Easter could no longer tolerate her situation. Those two women probably should have minded their own business as well, but they were too kindhearted for that, and too smart to tell their husbands what part they had played in Ruth Blackbird Hill's living at Lysander's farm. In truth, they had nearly forgotten about her themselves. Then, one day, Easter West found a pail of milk at her back door. As it turned out, Susan Crosby discovered the very same thing on her porch—cool, green milk that tasted so sweet, and was so filling, that after a single cup a person wouldn't want another drop to drink all day. Susan chose to go about her business, but Easter was a more curious individual. She couldn't stop wondering about Ruth. That night, Easter dreamed of blackbirds, and of her husband, who was out in the Middle Banks fishing for mackerel. When she woke she had a terrible thirst for more fresh milk. She went out to the farm that day, just to have a look around.

There was Ruth in the field, riding that old horse Domino, teaching him to jump over a barrel while the cows gazed on, disinterested. When she saw Easter, Ruth left the horse and came to meet her at the gate. That past night, Ruth herself had dreamed of tea, and of needles and thread set to work, and of a woman who was raising three sons alone while her husband was off to sea. She had been expecting Easter, and had a pail of milk waiting under the shade of an oak tree. The milk was greener than ever, and sweeter than ever, too; Easter West drank two tin cups full before she realized that Ruth Blackbird Hill was crying.

It was near the end of summer. Everything was blooming and fresh, but it wouldn't last long.

"What is it?" Easter said. "Does he make you work too hard? Is he cruel?"

Ruth shook her head. "It's just that I'll never get what I want. It's not possible."

"What is it you want?"

There was the scent of cows, and of hay, and of smoke from the blacksmith's shop. Ruth had been swimming in the pond behind the house earlier in the day, and her hair was shiny; she smelled like water, and her skin was cool even in the heat of the day.

"It doesn't matter. Whenever I want something, I don't

get it. No matter what it might be. That's the story of my life."

When Easter was leaving, Lysander Wynn came out of his shop. He was leaning on his crutch. He wanted something, too. He wasn't yet thirty, and his work made him strong in his arms and his back, but he felt weak deep inside, bitten by something painful and sharp.

"What did she tell you?" he asked Easter West.

"She's afraid she won't get what she wants," Easter said.

Lysander thought this over while he finished up working. He thought about it while he made supper, a corn-and-tomato stew. When he left Ruth's dinner on the stair he left a note as well. *I'll get you anything you want.*

That night, Lysander dreamed he wouldn't be able to give Ruth what she asked for despite his promise. She would ask for gold, of which he had none. She would demand to live in London, on the other side of the ocean. She would want another man, one with two legs who didn't spit out halibut teeth, who didn't fear rain and pond water. But in the morning, he found a note by the anvil in his shed. What she seemed to want was entirely different from anything he had imagined. *Bring me a tree that has pears the color of blood. The same exact color as my shoes.*

The next day, Lysander Wynn hitched up his horse to a wagon and left on the King's Highway. He went early, while the cows were still sleeping in the field, while the blackbirds were quiet and the fox were running across the sandy ruts in the road. Ruth knew he was gone when she woke because there was no smoke spiraling from the chimney in the shed; when Edward Hastings came to get his horse shod, no one answered his call. Ruth Blackbird Hill took care of the cows, then she went into the shed herself. She put her hand into the ashes—they were still hot, embers continuing to burn from the day before. She thought about red grass and burning trees and her parents calling out for her to save them. She kept her hand there, unmoving, until she couldn't stand the pain anymore.

He was gone for two weeks, and he never said exactly where he'd been. He admitted only that he'd been through Providence and on into Connecticut. What he didn't say was that he would have gone farther still if it had been necessary. He had no time frame in mind of when he might return. He would have kept on even if snow had begun to fall, if the orchards had turned so white it would have been impossible to tell an apple tree from a plum, a grapevine from a trellis of wisteria.

Lysander planted the pear tree right in front of the house. While he was working, Ruth brought him a cold glass of milk that he drank in a single gulp. She showed him her burned hand, then she took off her shoes and stood barefoot in the grass. Lysander hoped what he'd been told in Connecticut was true. The last farmer he'd gone to was experienced with fruit trees, and his orchard was legendary. When Lysander had wanted a guarantee, the old farmer had told him that often what you grew turned out to be what you had wanted all along. He said that there was a fine line between crimson and scarlet, and that a person simply had to wait to see what appeared. Ruth wouldn't know until the following fall whether or not the pears would be red, nearly a full year, but she was hopeful that by that time she wouldn't care.

# THE TOKEN

MOST PEOPLE WEAR BLACK FOR MOURNING, but my mother wasn't like other people. When my father died she tinted all our clothes red, from the tree sap we called dragon's blood. She dyed the leather of my shoes, to match her scarlet boots. She made a pie with her favorite red pears, and after she had eaten every crumb, she cried red tears. She tied our father's blacksmith anvil to our two cows and had the startled creatures pull it into the pond; when the mud splattered up, it was red as well.

I was eleven, but my sister, Ruby, was only a baby, little more than a year. She didn't speak yet, not a word, but even Ruby could tell how wrong it all was. My sister's hair was red like mine, but she was quieter; now she wanted to be held all the time, and she often made a whimpering noise, like a mourning dove. We had been pulled inside out by my father's death, our sorrow and our blood there for anyone to see, in our hair, our boots, our clothes, our pies, our very names. People in town used to think my mother was a witch; now that talk started up again. There was suspicion that my mother had dug up my father's grave; that she'd burned what was left of him on a pyre made of oak branches so she could keep his ashes under her bed. A witch without love was dangerous. Everyone knew that. People tried to talk to my mother, and in response she spat on the ground; she tore at her own flesh so they could all see how red our world had become.

My baby sister was my doll to play with, but she was also my responsibility. All the while my father was dying, from influenza and fever, I covered Ruby's ears, so she couldn't hear my mother sobbing, then weeping, then cursing our world. I sang Ruby songs about stars in the sky and about true love; I sang about the gates of heaven and about a pony who always knew the way home. I kept my sister even closer when my mother started bringing our belongings out of the house with that look on her face, the one I had grown to recognize meant, *Stay away*.

A desk went first, then a table, then our Sunday clothes; anything she could get her hands on. Blankets, yarn, flour, tea, all of it heaped in a huge pile on the shore of our pond. I was smart enough to take the few things my sister and I cared about and hide them behind the lilac hedge. Ruby's little poppet doll and a spoon with a lamb carved into the handle; a silver bracelet my father made for me when I was born and my blue dress, the prettiest in town, the one my mother had spent weeks stitching, back when she could see colors other than red.

We were sleeping on the bare floor by then. Our beds were on the pile beside the pond, along with our quilts, our clothes, our everything. Every night we listened to my mother crying. We got so used to it that now Ruby woke only when the wailing stopped. We were like people who lived in a windy country, and then one day the wind stops. Suddenly, there's only silence, and that's far worse than the wind. We were about to take another bad turn. I could feel that in the silence, in the way my mother was disappearing, inside out, unraveling one red thread at a time.

One evening when I went to look for my mother, she wasn't in her room. She'd left behind our last blanket, dotted red along the edges, as though she'd been picking at her skin. There was a tin box in the corner, and I wondered if my father was in there, his bones carefully wrapped in red ribbon. Because my father was a blacksmith, his skin was always hot. Even in November or January, if he held you near you forgot about snow and ice. I was afraid I would cry if I thought about my father for too long. I was afraid my tears would be red, and then I would be lost. I would be like my mother.

I carried my sister outside, even though it was cold, the air forming crystals when we breathed out. People said our mother was a witch because she'd known bad fortune. Her parents had died in the last epidemic, her house had burned down, and now she had lost the person she'd loved best in this world. She went back to what she'd always known, and that was fire. She had started with kindling, baskets of dried peach wood and pitch pine. While my sister and I were sleeping on the bare floor, our mother had built a huge pile out of our belongings; it was just starting to burn. I went to the window to watch. The fire was blue at first; then, in a wink, it turned red. When I saw that color, it went through my heart. I had red hair, like my sister, and so I was called Garnet. Worth less than a ruby, but red all the same. Now I wondered if people whispered things about me when I walked into town; I wondered what they said when my back was turned. As I stood there, holding my sister, watching nearly everything we owned burn, I realized I would have to be careful about who I became.

By the time my mother was through, there was such a huge bonfire that men from five farms had rushed to our property to help put it out; they lugged pond water all through the night. Those men stared at my mother in her red widow's dress; surely some of them wished they had a woman who loved them the way my father had been loved, but they didn't say a word. When it was all done, Ruby had cinders in her strawberry hair. My mother's skin was streaked with smoke. My red shoes were covered with a black film that had to be scrubbed, hard.

My mother stayed beside the pond when the men went away, so I fed my sister breakfast. It was November, and there was very little difference between the color of the air and that of the ground. I had a feeling in my stomach that my mother would never walk back inside our house. Ruby and I picked the last few blackberries, but when we brought some to my mother, she wouldn't eat. She looked at me, and I could see the panic in her eyes. She could not believe that the world could still exist without my father. Her eyes were red, her clothes were red; she was bleeding right into the ground, disappearing. If I didn't do something, I would lose both my parents. I would be just like my mother, an orphan, a witch. I already had the red shoes. I already knew what she felt. I waited for the next bad thing. I tried to be ready, to invent a plan, but that's not so easy when you don't know what you're planning for.

Not long after, my mother found a cardinal. She killed it, then propped up its body with a stick in our yard. This was bad. More red, more blood. When it rained, the bird turned bright as a heart. As night fell, the cardinal's drab partner fluttered around the yard, chirping, hopeless. All at once, I saw what my mother was thinking. I saw it as clearly as though it had been written on her forehead with dried blood. If the cardinal's mate died of heartbreak, then my mother would do so as well. She would do away with herself, one way or another. I saw the look in her eye; I saw her red boots and the skirt that had once been dove-colored but was now scarlet. I understood that she might do away with my sister and me as well.

My plan started to form around leaving. I had heard about California. Eli Crosby had an uncle who'd gone there, and he'd written back that the grass was yellow; November was as hot as summer. Here, November was brown with a blood-red center. You could see your breath turn to smoke in the air. There were winterberries turning plummy already, but my mother was still sleeping on the shore of the pond in her red dress, beside a pile of ashes.

I started to think about California more and more, and how Ruby and I could get there. We would have to leave my mother behind; she was like a bitter ember, she would burn us alive. Still, she was our mother. How could we desert her? Sometimes she would cry all through the night and we would hear her. There'd be a puddle of red around her in the morning, so that the fallen leaves nearby turned scarlet. She'd gaze at me and at Ruby, and I'd feel frightened in a deep way that I couldn't begin to explain. Was this love? Was this what happened to you? By then, the cardinal's wife was perched in the lowest branch of our pear tree. Even when I chased her, she wouldn't fly away. She didn't make a noise, not a chirp, nothing.

When the doctor came to town on the fifteenth of the month, I went to talk to him, but he told me to mind my manners and do as my mother said. I visited the pastor, but he only advised me that death was a veil we could not hope to understand, nor were we meant to. I had to carry Ruby everywhere we went, and she was heavy. I had walked all the way into town that day and now there was all the way back to be dealt with. I had blisters, and the wind was cold. I sat down at the side of the road. Ruby had fallen asleep, and sleeping babies are even heavier than fretting ones. I had a cracker in my pocket, and I broke it in half—half for me, half to save for Ruby. I saw someone coming down the road then. I wished with all my heart it was my father, but it was only an old woman, selling pots and pans kept tied to her back with lengths of rope. She sat down beside me, and before I could think I gave her the other half of the cracker.

I told the old woman about my mother as she ate. She chewed carefully and she listened carefully, too, even though she was very old, maybe even a hundred; she had walked all the way across Massachusetts, from Stockbridge, selling her pots and pans. I told her how my mother was turning into blood, how she was basing our future on the fate of a cardinal, how my sister still wasn't speaking when other babies her age had mouthfuls of words.

"This is what you do," the old woman said. "Take whatever is most precious to your mother and bury it somewhere on your property. In exchange you will find what you need."

Of course the old lady wanted payment in return for her advice. She was a businesswoman, after all. She stared at my sister, her sleeping form, her red hair, the way her cheeks puffed up when she breathed in. I didn't like the way she was looking at Ruby.

"You can't have her," I said. "She's what's most precious to my mother."

"Luckily, that's not true. Otherwise you'd have to bury your own sister in the dirt. If this little girl was so precious to your mother, why would she be here with you? No. Anyway, she's not what I want. I'll take your shoes."

I slipped off my boots that had been dyed red on the day after my father left this world. The old woman took off her torn boots, stuffed with papers and felt, and slipped on mine. They fitted her perfectly. She laced them up, then did a little dance, so that the pots and pans clanged on her back. My sister woke up and laughed at the sight; she waved when the old woman went off, and I hoped that, after walking so far, she wouldn't be disappointed when, in a few miles, she reached the end of Massachusetts, the farthest shore.

I walked home barefoot. The fallen leaves and pine needles were soft under my feet. Softer than my boots had ever been. Along the road the stone walls were covered with red and brown lichen. I could taste November in the air. I thought about what was most precious to me in the world, the things I had hidden away when my mother collected our belongings for burning: my blue dress, my silver bracelet, my sister's spoon and her doll. Worthless, really. Not much better than pots and pans tied up with rope. "I have a pony," I sang to my sister, and she hummed along. "He's black and white and very strong." Ruby tried to pull off her red stockings; she wanted to be just like me.

When we got home, we found that one of our neighbors had left us a pail of potatoes for our supper. There was the lady cardinal, sitting in the grass, brown as pine needles. She didn't fly away when Ruby chased her, and I had to pick up my sister and carry her inside. When I closed my eyes, I could still feel my father in this house. That was why my mother was sleeping in the open air, tearing at her skin. For the life of me, I couldn't figure out what was precious to her. Certainly not Ruby. Not me. And then I knew what it was. A necklace of halibut teeth she wore around her neck. It had belonged to our father. The halibut had bitten off his leg, and for years after, my father would spit up fish teeth that had been left in his skin. They were cool when you touched them, like ice, like glass. They were the thing I had to bury deep in the earth.

That night, I left my sister sleeping. I was grateful that the moon was waning. It was a red slice in the night, and the light it cast was dim. The male cardinal looked black in the darkness; he'd been dead for some time, still he looked like he might fly away. I went out to the woods, my feet bare. I was as quiet as the mice who lived in the tall grass. A red mouse, with my red hair pulled back. My mother was sleeping beside a log where the possums lived. She hadn't eaten for days. Her eyes were closed tightly and her breathing was heavy. I knelt down next to her and I realized I was afraid of her. Even though she'd brought me up, and kissed me good night; even though she was my mother. I understood why people in town had thought she was a witch. There was no difference between her inside and her outside, no barrier, no bone, only blood.

I unclasped the necklace. I held my breath. I begged to be a mouse for one moment more. *Dream of leaves*, I begged of my sleeping mother. My head was pounding so hard I feared the sound alone would wake her. *Dream of falling oak leaves, red and brown. If they touch you, you won't wake. You'll dream on.*

The moment I had the necklace, I ran. I ran so fast and so hard there might have been a dragon behind me, but there were only falling leaves. I found a spot in the farthest field, where the turnips grew. I took the necklace apart. There were thirteen teeth, and each one felt cool in my hand. I dug the first hole. I thought I might find a turnip or a stone, but in the red moonlight something glittered. Something red. My father had told me that, a long time ago, the sailor who'd owned this house had drowned. Afterward, it was said, sailors' wives came here and gave offerings, whatever was most precious, to ensure their husbands' good fortune.

I got down on my hands and knees. I dug hard even though the ground was cold and my fingernails bled. I made a furrow, the way my mother did when she planted seeds. I found twelve red stones in all, rubies brought back from the West Indies. In exchange I buried twelve halibut teeth. The thirteenth stone was green, an emerald, the largest of all. In the morning I packed our few belongings into a leather bag. I combed my sister's red hair, and she laughed, and said "Ruby." I was glad that her first word was her own name. I had been teaching it to her all along, just so she'd know exactly who she was.

When we went outside, I found the cardinal's wife dead on the grass. Bugs had gotten into the carcass of her mate, and there was little left of him but feathers. I took two feathers, for luck, good or bad, time would tell. Then I tossed the female cardinal into the woods. She looked like a fallen leaf, brown and small and paper thin.

When we got to the pond, my mother was awake, but she wasn't moving. She had found the halibut-tooth necklace gone, and had scraped at her neck until there was a line of blood, a crimson necklace, blood hot, burning.

"You," she said to me, as though I were her enemy.

I wasn't barefoot anymore. I'd put on some old boots I'd

found in the back of my father's closet. They were mis-
matched, but I didn't care. If someone were to look at me,
it would be because I was smart. Because my hair was so
red it appeared that my inside was the same as my outside;
no barrier, no bone, only blood.

I crouched down and opened my hand to show my
mother what I'd found. I wasn't afraid of her anymore. I
told her we were going to California. We were going some-
place where November was as hot as July, where the grass
looked like gold; we were taking what the sailors' wives had
left us and accepting the jewels as our good fortune. What
she decided was up to her.

My mother thought it over. Faster than I would have
imagined, she agreed to leave with us. But she had a price.
Didn't everyone? I sat back on my heels and waited to hear
her bargain. She wanted to take the two things she cared
most about with us; she wouldn't leave them behind. I
thought I would have to dig up the halibut teeth, or take a
branch of the tree that bore red pears, or bring along one
of the cows, or carry the tin of bones that was left in the
corner, but instead my mother took my two hands in hers,
and then she was ready to go.

# INSULTING
# THE ANGELS

O<small>N THE FARTHEST EDGES OF THE CAPE, IT</small> was widely believed that cranberries first came to earth in the beak of a dove. If that was indeed true, then heaven was red, and the memory of paradise could be plucked from the low-growing shrubs that grew in the dampest, muddiest bogs—a far cry from heaven, it would seem, at least to some.

To Larkin Howard the bogs were heaven and earth and everything in between; he had worked harvesting cranberries from the time he was twelve, and his hands were permanently dyed red. That he would be marked in this way embarrassed Larkin, for he was a shy man, mortified by his own clumsiness. He rarely spoke, not even to the Dills, where he boarded, or to the neighbors who had known him since he was an orphaned child. He wore gloves to cover his stained flesh when he went to the meeting house or the tavern, no matter the weather. He even wore gloves to the barbershop on Main Street when he went in for a haircut and a shave. The barber, Max Jeffries, had a pet squirrel who would spin in a circle and whenever he came in, Larkin always made certain to give the squirrel a handful of dried cranberries he kept in his pocket.

Larkin was only twenty, but his family had died in a house fire, and since that time Larkin had worked for any farmer who would hire him, in any bog, and he never complained. He wasn't the sort to think about everything he didn't have, even when an employer cheated him, even when he worked all summer and fall with little to show for his labor but his red hands and his board paid in full. That was Larkin; he'd learned to make do, though that meant ignoring the harsh realities of his life. He put away the loneliness that had surfaced inside him the year he lost his family. In doing so, he put away other things as well. He looked past anything he didn't want to see, and therefore he often didn't recognize the truth even when it was staring him right in the face. Those cranberries he fed the barber's pet squirrel, for instance, were so bitter the squirrel always spat them out the moment Larkin left the shop.

Sometimes, on his way to work, so early that the black-birds weren't yet awake, Larkin would make a detour, and wander down a leafy lane to an abandoned farm he especially admired. The hedges were overgrown and the rooms were empty, but the place reminded him of the house where he'd grown up, the one that had gone up in flames when a kerosene lamp fell over unnoticed. He breathed in deeply when he stood there in the high grass. He had to force himself to turn away, but turn away he did, each and every time. He had no expectations; he didn't think about the day that would follow the one he was living. It might have been that way forevermore, until he was an old man too crippled by the cranberry scoop to manage a spoon up to his mouth, too bent by tending those low-growing bushes to stand upright, if he hadn't met up with Lucinda Parker on the day the blackfish came ashore.

It was a pink morning, misty, and the tide was especially low. Beaching of whales often happened in the place where the dike road had been built, a marshy acre which in older times—the days before men and roads and even cranber-ries—had led directly from the bay to the ocean. This particular migration had begun sometime in the night. Perhaps the whales were misled by a full moon, a false bea-con shining off the dark water beside the dike road. Per-haps some of the blackfish were diseased, or one ill-fated turn was followed by scores of confused creatures search-ing for some ancient route their ancestors had once taken from the confines of the bay to the open sea. Whatever had gone wrong, the blackfish had accepted their fate with a low, keening song. It was a sound much like water, elusive, drifting in and out of people's dreams, frightening cattle, calling the gulls and hawks to circle over a landscape of death and misery.

Lucinda Parker had heard the whales' song best of all. She worked for the Reedy family, whose farm backed up against the marsh, and she'd never been an easy sleeper. As of late, she barely slept at all. She was housed in a room above the barn, and from her one window she could see flickers of water when the tide was high. Lucinda was long past thirty and too plain for anyone to bother with, except for William Reedy, who left his wife and family sleeping in the house and came to her room on nights when she least expected him. It was always a surprise to her, the way he thought he had a right to her, and she could never choke out any words in his presence, for fear she'd lose her home and what little of her reputation she could lay claim to. She could never say, *Stay away*.

Lucinda heard the whales' cries as she was sleeping. She woke in the dark and threw off her quilt and went to the window, and immediately she knew what she must do. She made her way to the bay the way dreamers navigate their way to morning, without thinking, unable to stop what was about to happen. The whole world seemed topsy-turvy. It was nearly dawn, but there was a moon in the sky, so big and bright it might have been a lantern. Water was sand, sand was water, and the beach was littered with over seven hundred blackfish; those pilot whales, which were so sleek and so quick in the water, were motionless now. The shoreline was thick with the dying and the already dead, with pools of moonlight and eelgrass and the sorrowful sound of the thrush, waking in their nests. And there it was, that watery song that had awakened Lucinda. The marsh seemed to reach on forever, with the tide so low none of the blackfish could possibly survive.

Lucinda Parker, who was wearing nothing but her nightdress and a pair of old leather boots, cut across the marsh despite the chill in the air. She sank to her knees in the face of what was so mighty, so inevitable, so filled with sorrow. She wore her long, dark hair braided in a single plait down her back. Already, there were strands of gray. Perhaps people in town thought she was too old and too ugly to really be a woman, to have a man use her for his own pleasure, to create life. No one had noticed when her waist grew larger; sometimes she wept when she came into town to buy groceries for the Reedys, but no one bothered to ask about her troubles. She was ugly; what was a pinch more of ugliness? She was plain and fat; what was a little more added to her girth? She'd gone out to the cow shed three nights earlier, when she felt she was ready, so no one would hear her if she screamed. But she hadn't screamed, hadn't even called out, except to wish that the world would end, that the man who had done this to her would keel over and die, that daylight would never appear again.

Lucinda had the baby with her now. He was perfect in every way, hidden in a shawl so that he might have been anything, seashells found on the shoreline, asparagus picked from the garden, a dove fallen down from the sky. She unwrapped him and kissed him, though she'd been afraid to do so before, lest she feel anything. Now all she felt was emptiness, vast as the open sea. She carried him on a path in between the dying whales until she reached the low-water mark, where the reeds were as tall as bulrushes. The salt was so thick it looked like a crust of ice. She stood there in the moonlight, under the pink clouds, watching as the sun began to rise, breaking open the world into bands of yellow and blue, of daylight once more, inevitable daylight in a world in which there didn't seem to be any choices. Only instinct, the sort of action a desperate woman might take on a morning such as this.

Larkin was alone on the road at this early hour. He had his wooden cranberry scoop over his shoulder, where it rested easily; the scoop was a part of him, another arm, another hand, dyed the same red as his flesh. He smelled the blackfish before he saw them, and then the vision rose before him as he took the turn onto the dike road. The whales had already begun to rot, and the air was thick with mayflies and salt and a bad egg smell. Larkin thought he was imagining this odd vision, for it seemed that moun-

tains had grown up along the shore. He wondered if perhaps he had gone mad somehow, though he was known to
be one of the most reasonable and calm men for miles
around.

He took the first path that would lead him down to the
bay. With every step, he saw more clearly that what was before him was real. Hundreds of corpses, a fisherman's
dream, acres of flesh and oil, free for the taking. Already,
the dogs in town had begun to bark. Those few fishermen
who were left, old Captain Aaron and even Henry Hardy,
would soon awake with tears in their eyes. Could a gift
really come to them when it was least expected, a windfall,
a promise, a reason to get out of bed? It was a lean time,
and more than three hundred local men had gone off to
fight for the Union. Those left behind were old men, like
Henry Hardy and the captain, or boys like the Bern brothers, too foolish to find their way home let alone reach some
far-off battlefield. There were only a few family men left,
like William Reedy, who had to care for his flock of seven
children—eight, actually, at the present time.

The men in town were the ill, the wounded, the lame,
the overburdened; those who clearly could not be asked to
fight. Larkin Howard had something wrong with him as
well, though he looked well built and healthy. He was blind
in one eye and deaf on that side as well. He'd had a fever as
a child, not long after his parents died, and when it was
done and he'd risen from his sickbed, unattended to in his

lodging rooms, one eye was fine and the other was cloudy. Someone spoke to him, the lady of the house, Mrs. Dill, who expected him to work for his keep. Larkin had seen her mouth move, but he couldn't hear a word, not until he swiveled round to his left side.

Because of his failings, Larkin had never learned to shoot a rifle. He had never left town; never been to sea. He still had a ringing in his one bad ear. On this odd morning, he shut his cloudy eye and looked out at the bay. The pink light was striking the pools of water, turning them red. The tide still had a bit to go till it reached its lowest point, and more blackfish were being stranded as he watched. The smell was unbelievable. Larkin pulled his neck kerchief over his mouth in order to breathe. He saw the woman in her nightdress then, her braid down her back, crouched down in the mud. His first thought was an odd one: *She's been trapped.* It seemed to Larkin she'd been beached along with the whales, one of more than seven hundred, dying in the warming air.

Larkin felt the echo and the ringing in his bad ear as he ran down the grassy path, anxious to see what was wrong. The ringing was in his head as well. The smell was hellish, and the sound of the blackfish, moaning or singing, it was impossible to tell which, was like thunder, shaking the sand under his feet.

"Let me help you," Larkin said, or he thought that's what he said. But the woman must have heard differently, because, when he leaned down to pull her out of the mud, she turned and hit him as though he were about to attack her. She hit him a second time, and then a third, her arms flying. Larkin had to drop his cranberry scoop in order to protect himself. He pushed her off, trying not to hurt her. "Are you mad?"

When she fell away from him, he thought indeed she was. He recognized her as the hired woman from the Reedys' farm. Perhaps she'd been driven insane by this god-awful smell, by the pointless death of so many creatures. There was mud all over her nightdress, and her face was drawn.

"I just wanted to see if you need anything." Larkin bent to retrieve his wooden scoop, and that was when he saw the child. There in the mud, between two blackfish, it was crying, its little mouth puckered, fists in the air.

Larkin looked over at the woman, and Lucinda stared back at him. She didn't say a word.

"Can I do something?" There was that ringing, now in both Larkin's ears, the good and the deaf.

"You want to do something for me?" Lucinda stood up. She was black with mud, and she had the stink of the whales all over her. She had no idea that she was crying. "Change the world."

There were so many seagulls overhead, ready to feast on the dead, that before long everyone in town would know something momentous had happened. And it had. The baby looked up at a pink cloud; at last, he stopped crying. There was salt all over his skin.

"All right. Fine," Larkin said. "I will."

Lucinda Parker laughed, but it was not a pleasant sound.

Larkin pointed across the bay, to the farm he liked to look at and pretend was his on his way to work.

"Is that enough of a change for you?"

Lucinda closed her eyes. She could see the moon inside her eyelids. She could see all of the life that she'd led.

"I'll give it to you," Larkin said.

All he wanted was for the baby not to start crying again.

"Just take care of him until I can manage it."

Lucinda opened her eyes. She was still in the same world, and the baby was beginning to fuss.

"When is that exactly?" she asked of Larkin. "Never? Or the day after never?"

Poor Larkin Howard was a fool who was trying to stop the inevitable. How could he change anything? This was the bay of inevitability and of sorrow, of mistakes made and mistakes that were about to unfold, of all that had been lost in a minute or a lifetime. This boy, Larkin, couldn't possibly understand anything. Lucinda felt old enough to be his mother. She might have been if she'd had this baby long ago, when William Reedy first came to her, when she was only fifteen.

The baby in the mud was whimpering. He looked shiny, with the same slick, wet skin as the blackfish. If she'd ever had a child, one of her own, one she could keep, Lucinda would have liked for him to have blue eyes, like this one. Seawater, tearwater, skywater, blue as the heaven she'd imagined as a child, although truly that seemed another person entirely, that hopeful little girl who made wishes.

"Give me two weeks," Larkin said, "and I'll do it."

He was sweating. The day would be hot, and by now the fishermen in town were certain to be on their way. And yet, all of a sudden, it seemed as though nothing had ever existed but this moment. This one chance to do something right.

"Why should I give you anything?" Lucinda certainly wasn't making her salvation easy. "What's anyone ever given to me?"

"Two weeks." He was even more sure of himself now. "That's all the time I'll need."

It was a foolish promise, but one Lucinda Parker agreed to. Larkin stood there watching as she picked up the baby and cleaned the mud off, ignoring his cries. Larkin had to go on to the bog, but he felt paralyzed.

"I told you I wouldn't do anything," Lucinda said when she saw the way he was looking at her, as though he didn't trust her with a bale of hay, let alone a child.

She wrapped the baby back in its shawl. She could hide him in her room for a little while longer. She could hold her hand over his mouth if he hollered at night. She walked quickly, so she could get back before any of the family

woke, and as she climbed the grassy hill that led away from
the marsh, hurrying, out of breath, the oddest thing happened. She felt the baby's heart beating against her chest.
*Two weeks*, she thought, *and not a minute more.* All the same, she
remembered the girl she'd been so long ago, the one who'd
been hopeful, the one who had expected something from
this world.

LARKIN WAS WORKING IN THE MORTONS' BOG, OVER
in Eastham. By the time he had walked there he had decided to speak with old man Morton, who was full of good
advice. He waited until noon, when they sat down to the
meal that Morton's wife had made them. In the heat of the
day, with their fingers bleeding from the morning's efforts
of replanting, Larkin asked his employer what he would do
if he wanted a great deal of money, quickly.

"You're not thinking of robbing a bank, are you?" Morton laughed. His hands were red all the way up to his el-
bows.

"I would prefer not to," Larkin said so easily no one
would imagine that, now that the idea had been set before
him, he found he was open to considering robbery as an
option.

"Marry a rich girl," Morton suggested.

"None would have me." Which was true enough.

They were eating biscuits and Mary Morton's beans,

flavored with onions and lard. Larkin had been a good worker, and Morton one of the best cranberry men he'd worked for.

"Honest truth? There's only one way for a man like you to make fast money these days. Sell your soul."

Now it was Larkin's turn to laugh. Then he thought of the blackfish, already being cut up and divided. He thought of the mud, and of the baby looking up into the pink sky.

"Who would buy it? It's not worth much."

"It's worth three hundred dollars. One of those substitute brokers up in Boston would gladly pay you that. In turn, you go to fight in place of some boy whose family has enough to keep him home and safe."

"I've got the blind eye." Larkin was thinking about three hundred dollars and how he would never in his lifetime earn that much, how he would still be working other men's properties when he was as old as Morton.

"They don't give a damn about blind eyes if you're willing to go in another man's place. Hell, you could have hooves and they'd take you and they'd make you pretty welcome, I'd wager, if you were idiot enough to make a trade like that."

Walking home that day, Larkin felt less tired than he usually did. The air still smelled bad, but he paid no attention. He kept thinking about that three hundred dollars and the baby; it was as though he'd never had a thought before. His head was filling up with ideas, and there was nothing he could do about it, not any more than he could stop the ringing in his ears.

When he neared the dike road, he could hear the voices of his neighbors, and the song of the few blackfish left alive. The men had taken saws into the bay to set to work; even the smallest children were out there helping, racing over the muck with buckets and carts. Here was enough oil to last all year; the slim time grown fat with death. Larkin might have earned some extra money if he'd pitched in, but it wouldn't be enough for his plans. It wouldn't be three hundred dollars. The next day, instead of going to work, he went down to the town hall. He had never missed a day of work before, unless he had a fever; he figured that when Morton wondered where he was, never in a lifetime would he guess that Larkin was discussing buying that old farm he liked to look at so much.

He signed a promissory note that very day, although what he was promising he didn't yet have. That evening he bathed in a tub of hot water, and he scrubbed his hands until they were raw. They were still red, and perhaps they always would be, so he put on his gloves before he went out. He told Mrs. Dill he was off to the tavern, though he was headed in the other direction, guided by a moon that was still fat and so white it hurt a man's eyes to see its light, especially a man like Larkin, who could only see so far.

He managed to find the barn, half blind or not. It was a squat, unappealing structure, set so close to the marsh that

at full-moon high tide water rushed underneath the building, lulling the skinny cows and the one mule to sleep.
None of these creatures made a sound when Larkin let
himself in, or as he climbed up the steps to Lucinda
Parker's lodgings. She was sitting by the window, from
which she could see the silver splash of the high tide. She
was so used to a man coming into her room uninvited she
didn't even blink. The baby was in a basket that had been
used for chicken feed; there were little sunflower seeds and
suet sticking to his arms and legs. He threw his fists into
the air when Larkin leaned over the basket. The baby
looked stronger tonight. The kind of hardy boy any man
would want for a son.

"You've been feeding him well."

"I haven't got much of a choice. I've got milk dripping
so that I have to bind myself when I go out."

She didn't tell Larkin that she'd been letting her milk
dry up, painful as that was, offering the baby a rag soaked
with cow's milk rather than her own breast.

Larkin placed the basket on the floor; he bent and let
the baby try to catch his finger.

"I signed a note for the farm across the bay. I'm taking
the steamer into Boston tomorrow to collect the money."

Lucinda snorted. She had reason to be nervous. What if
Reedy came tonight and found out about the baby? She
was supposed to get rid of it, but here it was still in the basket. What if Reedy hit her in front of this boy, Larkin?

What if he hit the boy instead? Lucinda knew how to use a rifle; her brother had taught her before he'd run off, leaving her to fend for herself. If she'd had a rifle still, she'd be happy to shoot William Reedy dead without a second thought if he came after them.

"Who'd be foolish enough to give you money?" Lucinda grabbed the basket and moved it back beside the bed. When the baby cried at night, she had no choice but to feed him, just to silence him, even if she did feel his heart beat against hers.

Larkin told her about the substitute brokers in Boston, and how he planned to sign himself over to serve the Union in exchange for another fellow's freedom; how he'd return on the steamer to pay off the farm so that Lucinda and the baby could move in.

Lucinda went to her bureau and took out everything she owned. A shawl, a prayer book, two skirts, the milk-soaked rags for the baby to suck on when it fussed.

"You don't think I'm letting you out of my sight, do you?" she said when Larkin seemed puzzled. "We're coming with you to Boston. We'll be with you when you get paid."

They left long before dawn, when the cows and the mule were still sleeping in the damp stalls, as the high tide rushed out from beneath the rickety foundation of the barn. Larkin carried the basket for the baby tied to his back; Lucinda had all she owned plus the child. They walked to Provincetown in silence, though it took them the best part of the morning. It was a hot day. The ruts in the sandy road were deep, better for carts and horses than men and women. Lucinda didn't really remember having parents, only her brother, the one who'd run away out west. Larkin reminded her of her brother, as a matter of fact, walking too fast, not bothering to talk, although he once pointed to the sky when red-tailed hawks were circling. The air was still acrid; whale fat was being cooked in kettles in the best part of three towns, and the stripped corpses left on the beach were baking in the sun.

At last they came to the rise from which they could see the harbor in Provincetown. Larkin gulped in the air, the cool, salt-smelling breeze from the north. He might never be back. Might never again walk down that lane where oaks and pitch pine grew, or gaze at that old house where a pear tree took up most of the yard, and the fields were overrun by sweet peas and meadow grass.

Larkin used his savings to pay for their passage. It was a rough crossing, despite the mild weather. Possibly the storm was leagues under the sea, some underwater catastrophe that had caused the blackfish to school in such huge numbers, then lose their way. Lucinda leaned over the side railing and vomited, but she didn't complain. Perhaps other passengers took them for a couple: the handsome young man who wore gloves, and the plain older woman with their child. Assuredly they were united in one thing, their goal of getting to Boston unnoticed.

Lucinda, however, didn't seem to trust Larkin. They took a room in an inn near the docks, but she refused to stay there and wait. Instead, she followed him to the address of a substitute broker on Milk Street. Even then, she didn't seem to want to let him out of her sight.

"Pretend you can hear even if you can't, so no one will think you're deaf. Get the money in your hand before you sign any documents," she told him, the way she might have advised her brother if he hadn't run off and left her, if he'd been the one trying to change her world.

When Larkin went inside to the brokers, Lucinda leaned up against the wooden building. She should have been exhausted. The sleepless night, the walk to Province-town, the six hours on the steamer, the walk to Milk Street. Instead, she felt as though something had boiled her blood. She felt awake for the first time. She'd never been to Boston, and she fell instantly in love with the city. The more crowded the better. Everything was glorious to her: the scent of horseflesh, and bakeries, and coffee, and tar. She held the baby over her shoulder when he cried and patted his back. She thought about the day when her brother left. He'd been given over to be raised by a farmer in Truro, while Lucinda had gone to the Reedys'. He'd had his rifle over his shoulder on the day he ran, and he hadn't been more than fourteen. She hadn't blamed him for taking off, not at all. If she'd been a boy, she would have done the same. She would have disappeared long ago.

Larkin came out an enlisted soldier in the Union Army, with three hundred dollars in silver, a uniform, and a rifle he'd had to pay for.

"They made you buy your own gun?" Lucinda drew him into a doorway so she could count the money then and there and make certain they hadn't been cheated.

When she was satisfied, they went back to the inn, where they'd registered as husband and wife. Larkin folded his uniform onto a chair, and placed the rifle atop the pile. Lucinda went down to a food stand on the docks and brought back fried fish and beans. After they'd eaten, Lucinda took off all her clothes and got into the lumpy bed. She hadn't had any sleep for twenty-four hours, and she needed some now.

"If he cries during the night," she said of the baby, "let him suck on one of those milk-rags."

Larkin stretched out on the floor, beside the baby's basket. The harbor was noisy, and shouts echoed from the taverns and the coffeehouses, but Larkin was so tired he fell asleep as soon as he closed his eyes. He dreamed about the farm, about tall grass and pear trees. He dreamed about cranberries. He could always tell when it was time to harvest from a tiny fraction of change in their shade—from red to crimson to scarlet. He heard something once, in the middle of the night, the baby whimpering, but before Larkin could rouse himself and get one of the milk-rags, Lucinda reached down and took the baby into bed beside her. Then it was quiet.

When Larkin woke in the morning, sunlight was streaming through the dusty window. The sound of the docks rose up, men and boats, crates delivered, teams of horses. Larkin felt a thickness in his throat. He felt some sort of strange loss. He had two days to report to the fort in Braintree, and from there he'd be sent on with his division. But all he could think about was here and now, this one morning, this one room. He sat up and waited for his good eye to focus. The bed was empty; that was the first thing he noticed. He felt an ache in his chest. Lucinda was gone. He grabbed his jacket and reached into the pocket. Now he was confused. The money he'd gotten from the broker was still there. He went to the window and looked out at the sea. The sunlight was blinding.

Larkin went to sit in the chair beside the bed to think things over, and that was when he saw the basket. He leaned over and looked down at the baby, sleeping, the tiny chest rising and falling. Lucinda had left her clothes on the floor, the homespun dress, the muddy underslip. She'd torn the bedding so she could bind her breasts hard against her chest before she put on the uniform. Then she'd cut off her hair and left it on the bureau. The color was pretty, gray and brown intertwined, like marsh grass.

Before he left for home, Larkin wrapped the braid carefully in a piece of muslin. A keepsake for the baby. Having
had nothing himself, he had a pure sense of what a child
needed, including that which someone else might find
foolish, the braid of his mother's hair, for instance. Walking along the dock, Larkin saw dozens of soldiers, some
boys so young it seemed they should be playing war in
their own yards. He was ready to go home and buy the
house down the lane where he so liked to walk; now that he
really considered it, he realized the boggy land around the
pond at the back of the house was perfect for cranberries.
He'd set to work as soon as he got home. Every day when
he stepped out his front door, he'd think about the blackfish that had risen up like mountains. He'd think about salt
and sorrow and the way he had walked along the road that
day with no idea of what the tide might bring in. When
people asked where the child living with him had come
from, he'd simply.say he'd found it on a battlefield. He'd ex-
press what he had come to believe, that some plans were
made not by men, or fate, or even heaven, but by circum-
stance, and by the song of whales.

# BLACK IS THE COLOR OF MY TRUE LOVE'S HAIR

IN EVERY STORY IN WHICH THERE ARE two sisters, one is always prettier. One wants the world served up on a platter while the other longs for nothing more than a rose. My sister, Huley, was the pretty one; you'd think she would have been selfish as well, but I was the one who was greedy. I wanted things I never should have begun to imagine I deserved. I was an ugly girl who lived in an old white house with my father and my sister, but in my mind I was something more. I read books as though I were eating apples, core and all, starved for those pages, hungry for every word that told me about things I didn't yet have, but still wanted terribly, wanted until it hurt.

My mother had named me Violet, most likely because of the blotchy thing on my face, a birthmark in the shape of a flower, blue in cold weather, hideous and purple in full sun; when the heat made me sweat, the mark stood out more than ever, bumpy and blistering, filling me with shame. My mother was kindhearted, but she died of a fever when I was seven and my sister was only five. I liked to think she was leaving me a blessing when she gave me such a beautiful name; I believe she assumed my pretty sister had no need for anything more than a name that would have suited a mule.

I did most of my reading in the barn, where our horses were kept. I thought of books and hay together, a single sweet parcel. There was no line drawn between the soft snuffling of horses breathing and the glorious worlds I most likely would never see. I read Greek myths. I read about far-off places, Venice and Paris. I read about men who searched for things they could not find at home, and women who fell in love with the wrong person and waited for the arrival of their beloved for so long that a year was no different from a single day. The same thing was happening to me. Years were passing. I was already a woman, and I still wasn't done reading. When my father and my sister went to sleep, I would sneak away from the house, taking a lantern. The horses didn't startle when they heard me. They were used to me. Maybe they enjoyed the sound of turning pages; maybe it made the taste of hay rise in their mouths. When I stretched out with my book in the pool of yellow light, I could hear the hum of the bees in the hive perched on the crossbeam above me—a thousand wings flapping in unison—and I'd think, *I'm alive. I'm alive.*

Our father was a fisherman, Arthur Cross, a good man, worn down by the sea and by the loss of our mother. He was often gone for weeks at a time, off to the Middle Bank, between Cape Cod and Cape Anne, along with his helper, a boy named George West. This year, when they came back from fishing at the end of August, George West had grown nearly a foot. He was rangy and silent and had blisters all over his hands. George was nineteen, a year younger than me, but he towered over our father. Although George barely spoke, and couldn't seem to meet my eyes—perhaps because he was afraid of the mark on my face—my sister and I were relieved that there was someone to help draw in the nets, someone our father could rely upon. When there was fishing nearby, runs of herring and bluefish, my father and George worked in our bay. Huley and I shucked razorfish and clams for bait. We harvested salt-meadow grass to feed our horses and the three dairy cows that were kept in the field. Books weren't the only things I knew: I could imitate the song of the red-winged blackbird that always announced the alewife's run. I could place a single blade of eelgrass between my fingers and whistle so loudly the oysters buried in the mud would spit at us. Still, all the while I was out there laughing with my sister, a straw hat on my head to protect my blotchy face, I was thinking about the barn, about books, about the yellow lantern light.

Before long, I had read everything in the schoolhouse, including *The Practical Navigator*, and had borrowed whatever I could from the lighthouse keeper's wife, Hannah Wynn, who had inherited a small library of books from her father in England. It was Hannah Wynn's husband, Harry, who first saw the serpent and filed the official report. Harry Wynn had been a surveyor for the county and a trusted observer of the coast for many years. Sea serpents of our local tales usually turned out to be whales, or large seals, or banks of curly seaweed, tangled and thick. Surely, there were strange things in the water; our own father had told us of a night when the ocean around his boat had turned green, as alight as the stars in the sky. George West had been a witness to this as well, if anybody dared to doubt our father's word. As for Harry Wynn, although he wasn't as honorable a man as our father, he wasn't a liar or a madman. Not in the least. People listened when he reported that the sea serpent was nearly fifty feet long, brown in color, snakelike in form, stinking of sulfur. Harry had watched the creature crawl out of the ocean, and, sure enough, when the men in town went to inspect the beach the next day, there was a trail in the sand, nearly four feet across. The smell of sulfur was palpable. Several men dropped to their knees, then and there, to pray for forgiveness for deeds they did not care to announce or explain.

One day everything was the same, the same sky and sea and beach, and the next day it was another world entirely. People saw shadows where none had been before. The women in town panicked. Most would not let their children wander freely; cows were brought in from the field, in case the creature had a taste for meat or milk; windows and doors were secured. An article appeared in the *Boston Post*, with quotes from Harry Wynn describing in great detail the size of the sea serpent's teeth, nearly four inches long, and the way it had looked back at him, before darting into the woods. By then, my sister refused to go to the shore with me, though it was only a mile from our door, so I went to dig up bait by myself. I wasn't afraid. I had read the *Odyssey* and I knew there was no way to escape your own fate. I knew that every monster had a beating heart, even those with scales, even those with flame-hot breath that could light the eelgrass on fire, even those whose faces were too terrible to see.

On the day the Professor arrived, we had what was called a spring tide, a tide lower than usual, so that the bay seemed devoid of water. I could walk miles out into the sea and find nothing but mud. There were enough littlenecks and quahogs to fill two wicker baskets. Before me appeared a world without water, and it buzzed with mosquitoes and gnats. It was September, that golden month. My straw hat made everything seem yellow: the mud, the sky, the sulfury shoreline. I saw the Professor from a distance, and, yes, my heart stopped. No one believes it when people say that, but in my case, it was true. It was just for an instant, but it was an instant I understood. Thank goodness I was wearing my hat. Perhaps he saw me as beautiful as he waved from the shoreline, my body young and strong, my hair in one long braid, nearly to my waist, my ugliness hidden by straw and sunlight.

His name was Ewan Perkins and he was one of the curators of the Harvard Museum of Comparative Zoology, a naturalist, originally from London, who had written for such esteemed journals as *Zoologist* and *Scientific America*. He was an expert in unusual creatures: giant snakes in Bolivia, a small breed of crocodile discovered in Oxfordshire, Mexican frogs that could not only climb but fly. These things I learned later, just as I learned he preferred toast with jam for breakfast, and hot, thick coffee when out in the field, but when I first saw him I only knew he was perfect. He was waving to me from the shoreline, accompanied by two men from the town council, Frederick Dill and our mayor, John Morse. I blinked, but if I wasn't mistaken the stranger held a book in his hand, a natural history of Massachusetts, at least three hundred pages thick.

"Well, that's a foolish thing to do," John Morse told me

as I approached with my baskets of clams. "You'll likely be eaten up in one snap if you're not careful."

"Unlikely," the Professor said. His voice went through me, as a hook might have done. No one in our world spoke the way he did, with such certainty and such clarity that a single word rang like a bell. "If the creature left the salt water, it's most probably looking for fresh water instead. Are there ponds in this area?"

I kept my head down so he wouldn't see my face. So I'd have a few more minutes of him thinking I was beautiful. Through the straw of my hat brim I could see that his eyes were some strange pale blue. I was done for, I knew that. I was trapped then and there.

We had half a dozen kettle ponds in our town, bottomless, with cool water, and probably another score of small ponds, like the one at the rear of our property, where the cows grazed on water weeds that made their milk turn faintly green in the bucket.

"I know where you can find every one of the ponds, even the hidden ones," I said in a thin voice. "I could show you." I was acting as though I had very little patience and even less time and would perhaps do him a favor if it suited me.

"She's a smart girl," John Morse said. "You could do worse."

I owed John Morse my allegiance forevermore after

that, and would go door to door when his term as mayor came due, asking my neighbors to reinstate him. The Professor said he would meet me in the morning in front of the schoolhouse; the mayor would lend him a horse, and Frederick Dill would take him in as a boarder to his fine house, which had a grand view of the bay. I looked up then, and if Professor Perkins was shocked by my face, he didn't show it. He was used to monstrosities, after all, curious as a matter of fact. He gazed right at me with those blue, blue eyes, and for an instant I felt unusual rather than deformed. Something to be studied, understood, learned.

I didn't care what my father said when he told me not to trust strangers; I went to meet Ewan Perkins so early in the day that there was still a sprinkling of stars in the sky. I took the horse I liked best, the one I called Swan. Swan was ugly and old, but steady. I was so dizzy with what I was doing, I needed something dependable beneath me.

Ewan Perkins was waiting when I got there—he had one of the Dills' horses and a jug of black coffee, along with a satchel of charts and equipment and glass specimen jars. We started out down by the lighthouse, where the creature had first been seen. I was wearing my straw hat bent low over my face. I could hardly breathe when we stood close together and walked along the sand. The marks of the sea monster had been washed away with the tides, but every once in a while Perkins would bend down and extract something from the sand, using tweezers. After an hour, he had found several scales, rather large and brown as the mud. I was fairly certain they were the scales of a good-sized bluefish, turned color in the sun, but I said nothing.

"Do you think monsters are a figment of man's imagination?" Ewan asked me. The sun was coming up, and he had offered me some of the coffee, still warm. I drank it and felt I was floating. I watched the stars evaporate into the lightening sky. Who was I to say what men might imagine?

"There are always authentic abnormalities," I offered. "And if it's part of the natural world, it is, by definition, natural." It was brave of me to say, even braver for me to look at him straight on, not hiding what was wrong with me.

We went to the larger ponds, one after another, five in all, and as we went along I told him the names of the species of trees he had not seen before, common things, like pitch pines and locusts. The mulberry trees brought from China he recognized, for he had been to China once. There he had seen a flying squid, which arose from the waves like a raven, as well as a two-headed fish that could keep one set of eyes closed while the other blinked open and shut. He might have been to China, but he hadn't been to the Cape before. Things here were new to him, and therefore interesting. I told him about the white blackbird that nested in our woods, a ghost bird people called it, but

I'd collected four feathers and they had proved to be entirely corporeal. I pointed out the tracks of a red fox, the thickets of winterberry, green as we passed them, but scarlet in the dead of winter; I told him about dragon's blood, the crystallized tree sap we used as a dye for quilts and dresses. He started to look at me in a manner I recognized: it was the way I looked at a new book, one I had never read before, one that surprised me with all it had to say.

We met each morning for three days in a row. I learned to be quiet while he looked for samples. He was looking for tracks, scales, half-eaten gulls or terns, any bit of evidence. I drank hot coffee. I didn't bother with my hat and let my braid of dark hair shine in the sunlight. I walked through the mud and pointed out bullfrogs. I drifted salt out on logs, hoping to entice the sea monster into coming forth for what it must naturally need, the essence of what it itself was, the dregs of the salty sea.

My father had every reason to be angry. I didn't care for the cows, and they cried pitifully in the evenings, so that my sister, Huley, had to go out in the field to do the milking, even though she was afraid of the monster. I forgot my errands, my chores, my life; the horses waited in their stalls for me to come and read by lamplight, but I didn't appear. In time, Ewan put his hand on my arm, then my shoulder, then my leg. He kissed me when I wasn't expecting it, and then when I was. I thought about water. I thought about salt. I thought that every monster who looks at his reflection in pond water sees only the black movement of the water and the pinpricks of starlight from up above.

What happened was my fault, of course. I should have let him go at the end of the week, when he said there was no proof that the sea monster, if it had ever existed, was anywhere to be found. I thought of all the places Ewan had been, and all the places he'd yet to travel to, and the way he had held me close and lifted up my skirt. When he was with me, he always put his face against mine, not afraid to touch me the way others were, as though I were poisonous. That morning, I went to the harbor, where George West was already at work on the nets. I knew there was a huge run of bluefish. By noon of that day, the bay would be swarming as the bluefish chased schools of mackerel inland to their death.

"Don't tell anyone you saw me," I said.

George nodded, and as soon as he turned away from me, I collected the bluefish scales that had washed up on shore. I held a match beneath them, singeing them slightly, so that they turned brown and sulfury, almost like burnt feathers, there in my hand. When I turned to go, I saw George West looking at me. He had been working so hard on the nets the bluefish destroyed in their frenzy that his hands were bleeding.

"I'd wager Harry Wynn didn't see anything come out of the bay. He has nightmares, and he wanders at night. I've seen him myself. Barefoot in the snow, screaming at things that aren't there."

"Do you know a lot about things that aren't there?" I asked.

"I know a bluefish scale when I see one."

This was the most I'd ever heard George West speak. I wasn't particularly interested in hearing more. I went right up to him, close, even though I was stinking of sulfur and fish.

"Promise you won't tell anyone."

Why did I think I had the right to ask that of him? And yet he seemed to think I did as well, because he nodded. I ran off before George could change his mind. I wasn't sure he knew exactly what he had agreed to; I wasn't certain myself. I rode all the way to the Dills' house with mud on my skirts and the sulfur clinging to me. I was thinking about George West's bleeding hands and the way people did strange and desperate things, and I got myself more and more worked up. The sun was burning hot, and my face hurt the way it did sometimes, as if something were stinging me, as though bees were under my skin.

Mr. Dill brought me into his guest room, where Ewan was already packing. There was the smell of lemon in the room, and of coffee, and of mud. I had wrapped the scales in my shawl, which I now laid on the bed. I watched as Ewan unwrapped them and I nearly fainted with nerves. I thought about his hands on me. I thought I could make a lie into the truth.

The look on his face when he saw what I'd brought him seemed worth anything.

"Violet," he said, and I wanted to shout out, *Yes, yes, it's me, I'm alive!* But I looked at the floor, as though I were frightened by what I'd found. I let the story out slowly; I knew from all the reading I'd done that was the best way to tell a tale, start far away from the center, but know where that center is at all times. For me the center was the way he was looking at me. He got overheated just hearing about the tracks I'd happened upon on our property. I said that for the past two days our cows had been dry; something with a taste for milk had been feeding from them, then slinking back into the murky waters of the little pond at the rear of our farm, crushing the last of the mallows, and the duckweed, and the plumy milkweed, whose feathery pods were beginning to rise into the air whenever the wind came up. Then, last night, I had found the scales. They were so full of the serpent's sulfur they had burned my hands. I showed Ewan the charcoal edges of my fingertips, where the match had spat at me while I was holding the scales of George West's bluefish over the flame.

Ewan unpacked his trunk right then. I helped him, if the truth be told. Perhaps Mrs. Dill, who was watching us from the hallway, thought this was overly familiar, but I didn't care. The story had a center and this was what it was: Ewan Perkins and I rode out to our farm that very day. We were there before supper. It was the time of year when the sweet peas have their last wild bloom. Our cows were crazy for them, and the milk they gave was especially sweet at this time of year. There was dust rising up from the road to our house, yellow dust on the white clapboards, milkweed spinning across the fields. My sister was out with the cows, trying to get them to follow her home, and Huley was golden as well. Her yellow hair fell down her back; her arms were bare. Even though I had seen Huley every day of my life, I could still recognize how beautiful she was. I didn't look at the way they stared at each other when I introduced them. I thought Ewan would laugh when my sister talked about how afraid she was of the monster, how she wasn't surprised in the least that it had wound up in our pond, it had probably been drawn to our property by the strong fragrance of the sweet peas. She heard things at night, Huley admitted, like a whispering, like the sound of scales dragging along the meadow. *You idiot,* I wanted to say, *that's me, reading, turning pages, being alive,* but I didn't say anything. I stood there thinking that sweet peas had no scent, at least not to me.

My father wasn't happy with the idea that Ewan would set up a camp on the shore of the pond. He didn't offer coffee or supper, the way the Dills had. My father wasn't the sort of man who was pleased when a reporter from the

*Boston Post* came to see the campsite Ewan put up—a tent and two kerosene lanterns and a little boat borrowed from John Morse. Soon enough, a story appeared announcing that a Harvard naturalist was convinced he would soon have proof of his monster right in our town. Already, he had found unrecognizable tracks in the weeds, headed toward the cows. There were whiskers—plucked from the muzzle of my horse Swan, and singed with a match—that had recently been discovered in the shallows of the pond. Surely, no fish, not even the catfish at the very bottom of the muck, had whiskers such as these, which was why Ewan kept them stored in a thin envelope. I was happy to row out to the center of the pond and sprinkle salt on the lily pads. I was happy to sit by the shore as a lookout far into the night. Sometimes, Ewan kissed me, but it was different and darker, and I let him do more to me all the time. I wanted him to; I put salt on my skin to draw him to me. I thought of him as I used to think of books, the thing that could make me other than myself.

I grew tired from the hours I was keeping. Up in the middle of the night to tend to the cows, then trudging through the winterberry to throw the milk away in order to claim the serpent was feeding in our field again. Making the serpent's trail with a snowshoe and a shovel that bent down the yellowing stalks of the sweet peas. Gathering scales from the last of the bluefish, which would soon disappear from our bay; it was the end of the season, after all, and the bay was colder with every passing hour. Wrapping my arms around Ewan until I all but disappeared, until the only thing that was left was the blotch on my face in the shape of a violet, the sort that lasts only a week or two in the spring.

I overslept one day, and after I'd pulled on my clothes, I ran down to the pond. I realized how much time had passed since Ewan had first come to town because the coot had begun to migrate, flying over town as they did every October. Things weren't so yellow anymore, except for my sister's hair. She had brought him coffee, and maybe she had been doing that for some time. There was nothing wrong in that, they were merely talking; it wasn't like the way we were at night in his tent, so feverish I could feel the salt rising on my skin. I could feel the mark on my face stinging with the thousands of bees that were inside me. It was something else entirely, the way he looked at her as he drank his coffee. I ran back through the milkweed. I had a hundred pods of it in my hair and stuck to my clothes, not that it mattered. I went upstairs to my bed and I stayed there. I didn't come down for dinner, I didn't milk the cows, I didn't do the work of my deception that Ewan had so come to depend upon.

My sister brought me soup, but I spat it on the floor. My father came to my bedside, worried, but I didn't even look at him; instead, I stared at the patterns of shadow on the wall. Ewan came to the kitchen for tea in the afternoons. I could hear him asking how I was, but I could also hear the tone of my sister's voice. After several days, I had a strange visitor, one I wouldn't have expected. It was George West, bringing me an apple cake that his mother had made. It was the time for apples, and the cake smelled good, but I turned my face away. That was when George West gave me the other gift he'd brought.

"I won't tell anyone," he said.

I looked at him then, and he quickly looked away. This time I didn't think it was because he was frightened by my face. I saw what he'd brought me: three bluefish scales, perfect, larger than any I'd seen before, already singed at the edges, sulfury and brown. I got out of bed then, even though I was only wearing my nightgown, and hid what George had brought me in the back of the storage bin in the wall. I was careful so as not to tear the scales; they were delicate, really, beautiful things. When I turned around, George was gone.

I kept the scales in storage, but I didn't look at them again. I could smell them, though, the salt and the sulfur, tinged with the scent of apples from the cake on my bureau. In the night I dreamed about bluefish. I dreamed that I was far out in the bay, in a world of water, at the very edge of the map. I dreamed someone I didn't recognize was drowning and there wasn't a thing I could do.

The next afternoon Ewan Perkins talked my sister into going out to the pond. He must have been desperate for proof of something, and she must have been desperate as well. She was afraid of snapping turtles and bullfrogs and hornets, whose sting could bring down a horse. When I followed them to the pond, I realized my sister looked like a splash of milk, a pool of sunlight. What a relief that must be to a man used to monsters. She was laughing, but I could tell she was scared that the serpent might be lurking somewhere close by. Among the many things Huley was frightened of was the water; she'd never learned to swim. Now I remembered that after our mother died I used to sleep in bed with my sister. I would promise her that her nightmares weren't real things. It was only her imagination, and she seemed to accept that as something less important, less powerful. Ewan was reaching for a water lily, the Egyptian sort, something yellow and glorious to present to my sister. He probably had no idea they were as common as weeds in our pond. Surely, he had no idea of how easy it was to trick a man, even one who was so devoted to zoology and nature.

My hands smelled like fish scales and sulfur and apples. I hadn't bothered to braid my hair, and it fell down my back, heavy and hot. I heard something in the sky, and I looked up, thinking it was some of the coots, traveling south, but it was that white blackbird, the one I saw now and then. I had never really found any of its feathers; I'd only said that I had. I kept walking toward the pond—pulled there, it seemed. I went up to my sister, and I pushed her, hard. She tipped over, in a single plash. The water was deep right away; she'd been standing on a bluff, the place where the milkweed grew. For an instant there was nothing. Not a sound. Ewan was standing there, looking into the water. His skin was so thin I could see his veins.

I jumped into the water after her, and the cold was a relief. My dress billowed out like a cloud, like a lily. I put my arms around my sister's waist. She smelled sweet. I remembered that about her. I wondered what it would be like to go where she was going, to walk through the streets of Cambridge and London, to be waiting while he traveled, searching for things he'd probably never find. I saw an insect walking across the water, a small miracle, perhaps, but a miracle all the same. I thought I'd just keep the fact of its existence to myself, or maybe I'd ask George West if he'd ever heard of such a thing, if he might happen to know its name, if by any chance he'd ever seen one himself.

# LIONHEART

*I*N 1908 THE FIRST AUTOMOBILE ARRIVED in town, driven along the sandy King's Highway, with the horn honking so loudly that sea fowl and hunting dogs alike took up the racket until the whole town was vibrating. Things shook and rattled and fell apart in a matter of minutes. Early McIntosh apples tumbled from the trees. Milkweed was blown off its stalks. Girls who had sat down to do their mending pricked themselves with needles and drew blood.

It was Jack Crosby who was driving the automobile, the Crosby son who made his fortune in oysters and lived on Beacon Hill, not the other one, Edward, who drank himself to death on his boat docked in Provincetown. Jack Crosby had initiated the Crosby Fellowship, which would send one local boy to Harvard each year, and the first recipient was Lion West, the smartest boy in town. The best-looking one with the nicest temperament, too, if his mother, Violet, had anything to say about it, and she was a woman of good judgment who had raised seven children in all, three other sons who were perfectly fine boys, and three wonderful daughters.

The children who followed Violet's firstborn, those wonderful daughters and fine sons, were Gemma, Susanna, Huley (after Violet's sister, who had died of fever while traveling in Egypt), George Jr., Seth, and John. Anyone would expect even the most loving mother to get the names of her children wrong every now and then, especially when there were so very many of them, to call for red-haired Gemma when it was dark, moody Susanna who was needed to stir the split-pea soup on the stove, to scold Seth for the window John had in fact broken. But Violet never forgot who Lion was. When the other babies were born they had squeaked like mice, but this was a child who had roared, and so she'd decided upon his name. He was not like anyone else, that much was evident, and he never would be.

"Are you sure?" Violet's husband, George, had asked

when she told him what the child's name would be. "It's a big name to live up to."

"That's all right," Violet had assured George. "He will."

The other children arrived over the next ten years, one after another. Dark or light, son or daughter, they were all embraced and loved. Still, no one took anything away from Lion. The other children had to share rooms, the girls in one, the boys in another, with bunk beds built into the wall. But Lion had a room all to himself in the attic, to make certain that when he entered school he could study in peace and quiet.

Not that Lion West was a stuffy scholar. Nothing of the kind. He was an outdoorsman from the start, and preferred skating on the pond or fishing with his father, George, whom he idolized, to classrooms and books. Being smart had just come to him naturally. He didn't have to work at it in the least. For penny candy or chores exchanged, Lion would gladly write up experiments for science class or solve mathematics problems for his younger brothers and sisters. But soon enough they stopped asking for his help. And that made sense. The West children knew what their teachers expected of them, and, even more important, what they were capable of. *Oh, you're Lion's brother*, the teachers would say. *You're Lion's sister. Well, you have a lot to live up to*.

By the time Lion was in high school, the mathematics

instructor, Mr. Grant, asked the boy to teach the more difficult lessons, so as not to embarrass himself in light of Lion's greater grasp of the material and his almost unearthly knowledge. After a while, Lion seemed to be speaking a different language. He didn't mean to. Surely, he had no desire to elevate himself above anyone else. He played ice hockey with his brothers and let his sisters tie ribbons onto him on May Day, even though he knew the girls aimed to dance around him chanting solstice rhymes. He cut blocks of ice from the pond with his father till his fingers turned blue; he took care of the horses and the chickens, he danced with local girls, he sneaked up to the deserted cottage on the bayside and shared drafts of ale and off-color jokes with his schoolmates.

But his involvement in such day-to-day activities could not change who Lion was. No one understood him. Not really. No one even came close.

"It's like this, Dad," Lion would say as he tried to explain mathematical problems to his father, the books splayed open in front of them on the kitchen table, columns of figures that were indecipherable to anyone in the household, save Lion.

George would laugh, impressed not only by the boy's intellectual abilities, but by his kind nature.

"I could describe a halibut to you scale by scale, but don't show me figures," George said.

Violet West was not surprised by any of it. Not how

tall Lion was, or how handsome, or how singularly talented. She had watched him as a baby in his cradle and had known then and there. She had held his hand when he was a toddler and been certain of it. Lion was meant for great things. This certainty of who he was, the clarity of who he could be, made Violet love her eldest son all the more. When George got up from the table, confused by advanced mathematics, calling himself an old dog who was long past the age of learning any new tricks, no matter how good a teacher Lion was, Violet waited for her husband to leave the room. Then she sat down with Lion. She let him teach her the solutions to some of the easier problems, and if mathematics didn't come naturally to her, at least she understood bits of his language. What he loved, she loved, whether it be numbers scrawled on a page, or hot apple pie; whether it be biology, astronomy, or green-pepper soup. Sometimes they would sit in the parlor together, both reading—in entirely separate worlds, to be sure, but joined somehow. When this happened, other people in the family couldn't bring themselves to disturb them. All that could be heard in the parlor was the sound of pages, turning.

The other children noticed the special connection between mother and son, but they didn't resent Lion. They felt sorry for him, as a matter of fact. They might not have been as smart, but they weren't fools. To be loved so intensely tied Lion up and freed them. All the brothers and sisters understood this, and they acted accordingly. Susanna, for instance, had no fear that she would break her mother's heart when she married at seventeen. George Jr., never much for books, knew no one would try to stop him when he left high school to work alongside his father as a fisherman. There was a camaraderie among the children, a ring of good fellowship. They liked games and challenges, ice hockey and relay races. One June evening they had all decided to play tag in the woods after supper. It was a warm summer night, and the fireflies were drifting through the woods. The children, save for John, who was only eleven, were all too old for such games, which made them all the more enjoyable.

Lion had come up the drive at this hour, thinking about his future. He had graduated from high school, and had spent nearly two years working with his father on his boat, joined now by George Jr. But then the idea of college had come up; perhaps Violet West had gone to the town council or perhaps the town council had come to her, the sequence of events wasn't really clear.

All the same, Lion seemed to be on the path to college. He had just been to Town Hall, directed there by his teachers, especially Mr. Grant, and by the mayor himself. Lion was twenty, a bit old to start college; still, he had applied for the fellowship to Harvard. He knew that Jack Crosby was shifty, that he'd taken over some of the older fishermen's oyster beds at a fraction of their worth. Crosby was said to disdain shellfish as disgusting and unnatural, choosing to serve only beef for dinner at his house on Beacon Hill. Whatever he was, Lion considered himself to be a fisherman's son first and foremost, and he carried a fisherman's resentment of the bosses who seemed to be taking over the industry. At the very last minute, as Lion stood there in Town Hall, told he'd be a shoo-in for the fellowship, he'd taken his application and folded it into his pocket. He'd have to think about it some more, he told the town officials. He'd need a little more time.

Lion was considering his future as he walked toward the house on the June night when his brothers and sisters were playing tag. Could he really leave home? Could he be elsewhere when the red pears ripened, when his father chopped ice in the winter, when they took their boat out on the bay in the early mornings as the fog was closing in to make the whole world seem made of clouds?

Lion could hear laughter weaving around trees as he neared the house, and several shouts of surprise from deep in the woods. Though the dark had fallen in sooty waves, he could narrow his eyes and make out several familiar figures. There was his sister Huley, in her favorite gray dress, running to hide in the barn, and Gemma, easy enough to spy with her red hair. There was poor John, tapped to be *It*, traipsing through the woods after his older brothers and sisters, doing his best, but never quite catching up. Hundreds of fireflies were rising from their resting places in the tall grass, the males burning yellow with desire. The summer constellations were appearing in the dome above them: Libra in the west; Ursa Major, the she-bear, in the northern sky; Virgo, the goddess, always watchful.

Lion stood there for a moment, gulping down the sweetness in the air. He realized that, although he heard his brothers and sisters shouting as they ran through the woods, he couldn't understand a single word they were saying. Here he was, at the age of twenty, a man with extraordinary talents, and yet he felt like crying. He wanted to be just like the rest of them. He wished for it desperately.

Violet found the application in his pocket on washday. She took it out, unfolded the paper, read it twice, then put it on top of the bureau in her bedroom.

"He filled it out, but he didn't turn it in," she told George when he came to undress.

"Maybe he doesn't want to go."

George got in bed beside his wife. They had been married for twenty years, enough time for him to know that, although her back was to him, she wanted to talk about this. George slipped his arms around her waist. His love for her felt heavy in his chest.

"He's meant to go," Violet said. "How could anyone not want to go to Harvard?"

George West had salt on his skin no matter how often or how thoroughly he washed. He thought about how he'd always wanted Violet, even before she'd ever bothered to look at him, how he'd admired the way her mind worked.

"I wouldn't want to," he said.

Violet turned round to face him. The room was dark, but she could see him perfectly well.

"Do you ever think about it?" She didn't like to bring up the subject, and she knew George liked it even less. There'd been another man before him, Lion's father. It had all been a wretched mistake, except for the outcome, which Violet had never regretted, not ever, not once.

"Never," George told her.

"How could you not?" As for Violet, she thought about it every day, even after twenty years.

George laughed. "I think about fish. I think about you."

"No you don't." Violet laughed. When she laughed she sounded like a girl again, but then she started crying. She tried to hide it, she turned away; all the same, George knew.

"I'll talk to him," George said. "He's my son."

It was a few days before George could manage to get Lion alone. Since George Jr. was now fishing with them, the boat was no good. The house was too crowded, the days were growing shorter, and so George asked Lion to go hunting with him.

"Hunting?" Lion said. They'd never done so before. "What would we hunt?"

"Muskrats," George said, as if it were the most natural thing in the world for two men who had never gone hunting before to suddenly go after creatures who did no one the least bit of harm and had no worth to anyone except each other.

Lion thought it over. He got his coat and put on his heaviest boots. It would be muddy out by Halfway Pond, the best area for muskrats, if that was what a man was after. They left early, while everyone else was asleep; they took the horses and rode down the King's Highway, then into the woods. There was a fellow who lived out here, old Sorrel McCluskey, in a cabin he'd built on town land, who'd pretty much hunted the place clean and wore a coat made out of the pelts of the muskrats he'd caught.

"Bad weather for hunting," Sorrel said when they stopped by his cabin to pay their respects. "Muskrats like fog. Foxes like rain. But a clear day's good for nothing."

Well, they would see about that. They were fishermen, after all. They had patience and plenty of time. There probably weren't more than two muskrats left in the area, but that was fine.

"Your mother wants you to apply for that fellowship," George West said after they had both gotten comfortable.

They had a nice view of Halfway Pond, but it wasn't any prettier than the pond on their own property. "The thing is, if I apply for it, I'll get it."

"I think your mother knows that."

"She doesn't know me the way you do, Dad," Lion said to his father. "The way we feel about this place."

George had brought along a breakfast of two ham sandwiches wrapped in kitchen cloths, and the men set to eating. It was so odd that George felt closer to Lion than he did to any of his natural children. Was it because Lion had been the first, or because Violet had needed him so at that time? Or was it simply because of who Lion was and always would be: George West's favorite son. While they had potato salad, George thought about telling him the truth—that George wasn't his father, that his real father had been a better man, a smarter man, a professor, as a matter of fact—but if George West was anything, he was honest, honest to a fault. To say Lion wasn't his son felt like a lie, so instead he said, "Well, she'd like for you to apply."

They didn't catch anything that day, but Lion brought his application back to Town Hall later in the week, and the entire family was proud of him when Jack Crosby came to town to present him with his fellowship. The whole town planned to gather down at the green on that glorious day, more to see Jack Crosby's automobile than anything else, but there all the same. Lion was to leave with Crosby—that was part of the hoopla—a ride all the way to Cambridge in this gleaming carriage, rather than the dusty old steamer that left out of Provincetown. All of Lion's sisters dressed up for the occasion, and George West put on his suit, the one he wore to funerals; Lion's brothers made a plaque, which they hung on Lion's bedroom door: *Here slept the first man in town to go to Harvard College.*

After George had sent the children on to the celebration, he got the horses harnessed to the cart and went to look for Violet. She was in the field of sweet peas that were all abloom, at their glorious peak. The goldfinch came here at this time of year, for the thistle. The crickets' call was even and slow.

George West leaned one foot up on the stump of an old oak tree. Something white moved across the sky, a cloud, a puff of milkweed, the snow-colored blackbird that lived up by the pond.

"Do you think I made a mistake?" Violet said.

She was not yet forty, but she was tired. She realized that this one August day divided the *before* from the *after.* All at once she knew that Lion wouldn't be coming back. She was right about that, as she had been about everything else. Oh, he'd visit now and then during his four years in Cambridge, but then he'd go on to Oxford, and he'd be given a position in London, teaching higher mathematics at the university. He'd be so concentrated on his work, so very busy, that he wouldn't even fall in love until he was forty-two, older than Violet was right now.

One day he'd be walking through Hyde Park and he'd see a young woman, an American girl, Helen, visiting an aunt and uncle, and he'd feel as though he was pierced through the heart. Nothing in the world of mathematics had prepared Lion for love. Nothing about it added up. He would think about the sweet peas back home at the moment when he met Helen, how they changed color depending on the sky, pale and pearly at dusk, pink under the noon sun, purple and violet and finally gray as the day disappeared.

Lion would send photographs of his wedding, of course, a small affair in a lovely chapel in Knightsbridge. He would send Christmas cards faithfully, birthday greetings to all his brothers and sisters, books he thought his father would appreciate, illustrated texts about fishing mostly, hunting occasionally, perhaps as a reminder of that day they went looking for muskrat.

To his mother, Lion sent a photograph of himself and Helen and the new baby, Lion Jr., framed in silver. They were poised in front of his MG roadster, his favorite possession. It was nearly impossible to see the baby's face, but Helen looked lovely and young, and there were glorious chestnut trees, and the roadster shone like a mirror. Lion had been a fan of motorcars ever since that day when Jack Crosby gave him a ride to Cambridge. It had taken the best part of the afternoon to get to the city, and the motor had twice broken down, but Lion had been won over completely. He especially liked the feel of the wind, the sense of flying, the way the trees floated by.

"This is the beginning for you, kid," Jack Crosby had told him. He'd had to shout so that Lion could hear him over the rattling noise of the motor. They were both wearing goggles to keep the bugs out of their eyes.

Every time he drove his car, Lion thought about that day. The way his senses had been heightened, the way he'd understood, all at once, what his mother had wanted for him. He thought about it when Helen and he went on holiday, their first after becoming parents, when the baby was three months, old enough to be left behind with a sitter. They needed a bit of time together, they needed the feel of the wind, the flying, the trees floating by.

"Not too fast," Helen said, even though she knew he wouldn't listen. Lion had a mind of his own. Always had. The chestnut trees were flowering, and there were roses blooming. The car was going so fast, the air felt like honey, warm and sunlit.

At home, their baby was asleep in his cradle. He had a wonderful temperament, and that was lucky for everyone. His babysitter would have to stay on, as it would be at least four weeks after the accident before his grandmother could come over by ship to get him. By then the child was sleeping through the night. If that wasn't luck, what was? He didn't make a peep. Not a cry, not a wail. He was absolutely lovely. One of a kind. A nurse could have easily been hired to take him across the Atlantic; certainly he'd be no problem. Even the sitter who'd grown so attached to him had volunteered. But Violet wouldn't hear of it. No one would make such a far journey with this child, except for her. Not as long as she had anything to say about it.

# THE CONJURER'S HANDBOOK

LION WEST, JR., WAS A MAN IN LOVE. HE thought about how this had happened to him at the absolute worst time in his life, and he wondered if that's the way things were in the world. A person thought he was headed north, only to have the ice melt away. He thought it was daylight, only to realize what he was seeing was the trajectory of stars in sky. Lion was already engaged to a perfectly nice girl from Boston when he was sent to New Jersey for his basic training; he was still engaged to her when he was shipped off to France, and then to Germany, there for the liberation. Lion was a mathe-

matician, like his father before him, but he had also studied German at Harvard, and was fluent enough to be
thought useful. He was steady and smart, and more than
anything, he was loyal. And yet, as time passed, that perfectly nice girl he'd been engaged to drifted further away
from him; she'd become Carol from Wellesley, her easy
temperament and innocence more and more of a puzzle,
considering the times they lived in. Her memory had been
replaced by the intensity of the things Lion saw all around
him each and every day: blood and sorrow, starvation and
terror, all kept pushing her out of his mind until she was
tiny and elusive, a firefly of desire. They'd seemed so perfect together and their future had seemed completely assured, and then, one day, he couldn't remember her name.

Lion was among the men who walked into a camp north
of Munich on an April day. They had a guide along with
them, a woman who could speak not only German and
English, but French, Italian, Polish, and even Yiddish, and
who could therefore say, *Show us to the dying, the children, the
lost*, in all those many ways.

"These poor people," Lion said of the people in the
camp. The idea of the sort of horror that could exist erased
everything he'd known before. What had he been thinking
all his life? What had he been dreaming of? Columns of
figures that always made sense, that's what he had always
admired. He was attracted to order in a world where there
was none, and now he felt empty. When the wind came up,

it cut right through him in some strange way that made him feel as though he were only half a person.

"I'm one of those people." The interpreter was a plain woman, a few years older than Lion, with sharp cheekbones and a wide mouth. "I'm a Jew. Do you have something you'd like to say about that?"

"But it's different, of course. You're our guide, not a prisoner."

The interpreter gazed at him; her eyes were gray, impossible to read.

"What does your father do for work?" she asked.

Surprised, Lion admitted what he usually kept private. Both of his parents had been killed in a car accident when he was only a baby.

"So much the better." The interpreter seemed pleased. "Now you have no one to lose. You should be thankful. Maybe you have a wife?"

Lion said no. He laughed at the very idea of ever marrying Carol now. The interpreter was wearing a rag of a scarf around her head, rough wool with frayed edges. When she glared at Lion he could feel the intensity inside her. "You think love is funny?" The guide came closer, so close he could feel the heat coming off her body, and it shocked him, like a spark. "I can undo any lock without a key," she told him. "If I had to, I could kill a man with a scarf."

Lion had always been the smartest and the best at whatever he'd attempted. He was the one everyone turned to for help, for advice, the favorite of all. He knew the answers to things, or at least he had up until now. Now he wasn't sure who he was. Was he someone who could stand on ground darkened by blood and not turn and run? Was he someone who fell in love at first sight?

He asked around and discovered that the guide's name was Dorey Lederer. She was their interpreter again, later in the week, while they interviewed children, trying their best to figure out what to do with those who'd been wrenched from their families and had not a single soul to call their own. When, after the best part of the next week, most of the children had been processed, the weather suddenly grew warmer. It was a joke of nature, perhaps, beauty and warmth in this wretched place. Now that there was no wind, Dorey took off her scarf and Lion West saw her head had been shaved.

"Did you have lice?" Lion asked.

"Everyone here has lice. As a matter of fact, you yourself have lice by now. You can't walk through the gate here and stay clean."

"I didn't know you were a prisoner here."

"I got out. I lied to everyone and anyone, but you can only get away with a lie for so long. Then you have to switch to another lie if you want to keep living. One minute you're a prisoner, then you're a soldier's whore, then you're a guide. I could be anything at all next. I know quite a few tricks. Want to see?"

She asked Lion for some money, which she vowed she would make disappear. Lion was already lovesick. What he felt for her hurt, it was brittle and hard and all-consuming. He could not believe that in a place so full of death he had found someone so alive. "Close your eyes," Dorey said. When he opened them again, she was gone.

But it wasn't so easy to escape from Lion; he tracked Dorey down. He wanted something from her. He wanted her in bed, but he wanted more: every secret she knew, every trick, every lie, every sorrow. She didn't say anything when he appeared at her door, and he couldn't tell whether or not she was pleased. Clearly, she wasn't surprised. She drew him into her room and let him watch as she took off all her clothes. She had two long scars; still, Lion thought he had never seen anyone so beautiful. "Look at this!" Dorey said. "I mean it! Really look. This is something I can't make disappear. Just so you know. So you don't accuse me of putting one over on you."

Lion pulled her onto his lap and he cried; despite everything he'd seen in the past few weeks, or perhaps because of it, he wanted her more than he had ever thought possible. He had never imagined people could treat each other in such barbarous and hideous ways. He had never imagined he could feel this way. He thought about Dorey as he was falling asleep and at the moment he woke up and during all of his daydreaming time in between.

"Sensitive men are useless," Dorey said one night. "I

give you the chance to get away this one time." She had her mouth to his ear and she was whispering; her every word made his head pound. "I slept with a man who was a murderer. What do you think of that? Disappear if you know what's good for you. Do it right now."

But it was too late. Lion had already begun to understand that he wouldn't be able to leave Germany without her; he asked her to marry him and come back to Boston. He would be starting a teaching position at Harvard. He was just an assistant in the mathematics department, and although it wasn't much, it was all he had to offer. He wished he could get her a big house in the country, and a horse like the one she'd had as a child.

"Give me your handkerchief," Dorey said. "I'd rather have that than a horse."

Lion did so, and Dorey quickly tied the silk in a knot around his finger. Lion tried and he tried, but he couldn't get it off, not until Dorey bent down and untied the handkerchief with her mouth.

"Now you belong to me," Dorey said, as if that hadn't been true from the start. "I feel sorry for you, really, because you'll never get away."

Lion was stationed for a while in Berlin, and when they went back to the States they moved into an apartment in Cambridge, near the reservoir, where they liked to walk in the mornings, early, before they had their coffee together.

When Lion's parents died, his grandmother had taken him in and raised him; she was the person who needed to approve of Dorey, the one whose opinion had always mattered most. Perhaps that was why it was so long before they went to visit her: Violet West was not one to keep her opinions to herself, especially when it came to her grandson.

Violet lived out at the old farm on the Cape, without heat or electricity; she still used the outhouse, and in the summers she cooked in the old shed so that the kitchen would stay cool. Lion had bought her a refrigerator, but she refused to have the house wired; she preferred to haul ice from the pond with some old haybag of a gelding she called Bobby and stack the neat blocks of green ice in the storage bin of the summer kitchen. Violet West had raised seven children and her grandson Lion. She had no fear of hurricanes or of loneliness; she hadn't once complained since she'd buried her husband of over fifty years when he passed on from a series of strokes. She was beloved in town, well known for making the best chocolate cake in the commonwealth; she was the head of the library foundation, and she knew every single plant that grew in the bog, from pitcher plants to wild orchids.

"What if she doesn't approve of me?" Dorey asked as they prepared for their trip to the Cape. They had already married, quickly, to make returning to the States easier.

Dorey had been employed by the German department at the local high school. "Will you divorce me? Will you throw me out on the streets? Even that won't work. I warned you you'd never get rid of me. Give me your key," she demanded.

Dorey held the key Lion gave her up to a match, then returned it. "Try it."

Lion grinned and went to the door. He slid the key in the lock, but it wouldn't turn. Dorey came over with a glass of iced water. She let the key float in the glass for a moment, then took it out and blew on it; when she tried it in the door, it worked perfectly. So perfectly, Lion had to kiss her then and there, even though when he kissed her he felt as though he were swallowing sadness. He knew he'd never be free from whatever this was between them, not that he wanted to be, not that he ever would.

Lion rented a car so that he and Dorey could drive out to visit Violet. It was late fall, November, and the weather was especially bad. They been busy setting up their apartment, starting their jobs, getting on with their lives, and it had taken them far too long to visit Lion's grandmother. Lion had a feeling of dread as the day of their visit approached: try as he might, he could not imagine the two women he loved in the same room.

Autumn had been colder than usual. The roads on the day of their visit were slick with ice, a light snow was falling, and the sky was swirling with clouds. Dorey's hair had grown back, but it was short and spiky and she looked younger than she was. Lion didn't think about her sleeping with another man, that German soldier, or anyone else for that matter, not any more than he thought of her taking food out of the garbage or putting her hands around an infant's neck so that the baby's mother would not be found out and killed. He didn't think about the two scars that crossed her abdomen, and if he happened to touch them, accidentally, she was quick to move his hands away.

"I know how to walk across snow barefoot and not get frostbite," Dorey said companionably. Bad weather and ice didn't faze her. She liked road trips. She liked Massachusetts. The dark woods, the fields of ice and hay, the way it was possible to get a good cup of coffee almost anywhere. "You have to concentrate and lower your blood pressure, and then the pain isn't so bad. It's nothing, in fact. Like a mosquito bite." Dorey had dressed up for the occasion of visiting Lion's grandmother; she wore her good black dress and the little diamond ring set in platinum that Lion had bought for her in Berlin.

"They probably took it off a dead woman's hand," Dorey had said in the shop. "It's easy to do, even if the flesh swells up. You just take a rock and smash the bones." Now she held her hand up and gazed at the ring, as though it were far bigger and more beautiful than it was. She smiled at Lion. "It looks good on me."

As for Violet West, she was expecting the worst. She

assumed that was why Lion had stayed away. She'd see the truth when she met this wife of his, and she'd have to tell him what she thought, simply because she was made that way. She knew how to test people. She'd made halibut stew and baked beans and molasses bread for supper, every dish she hated; she'd added handfuls of salt, too much pepper, just to test Lion's wife. She had stuffed the pillow on the dining-room chair where her visitor would be sitting with brambles and nettles and straw. She'd put stones in the bottom of the coffee cup at Dorey's place setting. She'd left the door to the outhouse open, so that ice swept through and anyone going inside would surely freeze her bottom. At the very last, Violet removed the board in the attic that blocked off the nest honeybees had made in the rafters. Lion and his bride would sleep there tonight, if they could.

Violet West did all this because she loved Lion in a way she loved no one else in the world, save for Lion's dead father, whom she had loved just as fiercely. She wanted everything for him, and no one could convince her that he wasn't entitled to all that was good in this world.

"I'm glad you don't love me like that," her husband, George, used to say to her. "I'm thankful. I really am."

"What are you talking about? You know I love you," she'd say right back each and every time. That was true enough, and yet it wasn't the same; it wasn't the way she had loved Lion, and then his boy, Jr., her grandson, the love of her life.

The last of the fruit on the old pear tree in the yard toppled from the branches when the car pulled into the long dirt driveway. Not a good sign, Violet was sure. If this had been another occasion, she would have already picked those few hardy pears and had a brown Betty or a red-pear pie in the oven, but there was nothing to celebrate, and molasses bread was good enough. Violet was standing out in the yard, waving. As they drove up, Lion was shocked at the state of the house: the white paint peeling off the clapboards, the chimney tilting, the old horse in the field snuffling through the ice, the pear tree so crooked its branches reached to the ground. He'd last been back for his grandfather's funeral, before he shipped out to Germany, before his world changed, and his grandmother certainly hadn't looked as old. He found himself fearing that she would slip on the icy path as she came to meet them. That she'd crack a rib, or break a leg, or worse. What if such a thing happened when she was here all alone? Who would rescue her? Who would know? The old horse, Bobby? Barney Crosby, who came to chop the fallen trees into logs?

"She hates me already," Dorey said just before they got out of the car. Even from a distance, she noticed the purple birthmark on Violet West's face, and she understood where some bitterness might have taken root. The imperfect were often angry; Dorey knew that from personal experience. "She'll look at me and see a Jew who stole you away."

"My grandmother's not like that." Lion's grandmother had taught herself algebra and geometry so she could help him with his homework. She had taken the bus into Boston with him when he applied to Harvard and sat in the bus station for three hours, waiting.

"Everybody's like that," Dorey said.

When Lion hugged his grandmother he had the sense of time flying by him, then and there, in the driveway. Violet's eyes were cloudy; her vision had been going and she hadn't told anyone, but of course what business was it of anyone but herself? When Dorey was introduced, Violet signaled her over, so she could get a closer look. Dorey surprised her by kissing her on the cheek, right in the place where her birthmark was. "Don't worry," Dorey whispered, "I'll share him." Or at least that's what Violet thought she'd said.

"You must be hungry." Violet took her grandson's arm. "Why don't you put Bobby in the barn for me?" she called over her shoulder to Dorey. "It will give me a chance to talk to Lion."

Lion looked at his wife, torn. There was Dorey in her good black dress with her high-heeled shoes. Here was his grandmother, leading him into the house.

"Don't worry." Dorey waved them on. "I'm good with horses."

Lion went inside and set the table, the way he always did when he was at home. But things weren't the same. The house was so cold, Lion kept his coat on. The dishes were all covered with a thin coat of grime. Violet stood by the window. The light was the blue light of November, a day that was ready and willing to shift quickly into night. She could see Dorey in the field where the sweet peas grew. Bobby was just about as stubborn as a horse could be. He bit, for one thing, and he always took his damned time. He was an unmovable, stubborn creature, which was most likely the reason Violet loved him. But, surprisingly, when Dorey clapped her hands, Bobby came right to her. She slipped a rope around his neck and led him to the barn.

"She knows horses?" Violet said.

"She knows everything," Lion told his grandmother.

Right away, Violet understood what she was up against.

"I've been cooking all day for you," Violet told Dorey when she stepped into the house.

The younger woman smelled of hay; she'd left her high heels, now covered in mud, at the door. She had learned it was always wise to carry a few packets of sugar in your pocket, along with a small knife, and enough cash to get you to the next town. She had learned that nothing was ever what it seemed to be. "I'll bet you have," she said.

When they went to the table for dinner, Dorey folded her coat and placed it on the seat that had been stuffed with brambles. She felt in her cup and slipped out the stones while Lion was getting the coffeepot from the stove. Violet West still used kerosene lanterns and heated the house with a single woodstove in the kitchen.

"You might be cold tonight," she told Dorey. "Lion's room is up in the attic."

"Oh, I don't think so," Dorey said. "I've slept with nothing for a blanket but a drift of snow. I've slept where it's so cold your mouth freezes shut and you have to concentrate in order to breathe. The attic will be fine."

Lion had often thought about his grandmother's wonderful cooking, and again he was taken aback. The supper was awful. No wonder Violet looked so thin and worn. She wasn't getting the right nutrition. She probably hadn't seen a doctor for a year or more.

"I'm worried about you being out here by yourself," Lion said. Dorey had insisted on washing the dishes; she knew how to work a pump and could clean a whole sinkful of pots with a smidgen of soap. "Maybe it's time for you to sell this place, and move into the city. You look tired."

Violet West was nearly eighty, but she was fine on her own. "Go to bed," she told Lion. "You're the one who's tired."

That night Violet fell asleep in the big chair by the woodstove. She hadn't mentioned to Lion that her eyes were failing, that her bones were so brittle the cold made them feel like cracking when she went out in the mornings to feed Bobby. She certainly hadn't brought up the fact that

twice this month she had nearly set herself on fire while
dozing beside the stove. Her sleep came in fits and starts
lately, it was true. And so at first she thought it was a dream
when Dorey came downstairs with the beehive. For one
thing, the beehive was cloaked in a white pillowcase. It
seemed for a moment that Lion's wife was carrying a circle
of moonlight, right across the kitchen. The bees were
noisy, the way they always were at night. Dorey put the hive
down on the counter and lit a cigarette. She was wearing
an old cotton nightgown, and her hair stood away from her
head in sleepy tufts. She blew some smoke under the pillowcase, and the bees fell silent.

Violet West sat up in her chair and blinked her hazy
eyes. She watched as Dorey reached into the hive and took
out a handful of honey. It was red-clover-and-sweet-pea
honey, the best there is on the Cape. There was enough to
fill a small crockery jar.

"I told you I'd share him," Dorey said.

Dorey went outside, barefoot, into the front yard,
where she lodged the bees' nest into a low branch of the
pear tree. In an instant she pulled off the white pillowcase
and ran back to the house. She smelled like honey and
clover. But her feet were blue with the cold.

"How much do you love him?" Violet West said.

Violet still had the feeling that she was dreaming. She
was so used to being alone in this house that it seemed pre-
posterous for her to be having this conversation with a

woman from Germany who was sharing her grandson's bed.

"How much do *you* love him?" Dorey said back.

IN THE MORNING, LION SWORE HE HAD NEVER HAD such a good night's sleep. It was even colder today; the ground was rock hard and snow was falling. Violet had made tea for her guest out of winterberries, which should have been foul enough to pucker anyone's mouth. Dorey added two spoons of honey and a packet of sugar from her pocket and announced that hot drinks in the morning were a gift from above. That was how Violet had thought of her grandson, a gift from above that she didn't quite deserve, but one she would care for as best she could. Lion said he was off to see some old friends in town; he asked Dorey to come with him, but she shook her head.

"Are you sure you want to stay here?" he asked when Dorey came to kiss him goodbye. He was going to talk to Nate Crown, who ran the real-estate office, to discuss what it would take to sell the house. Maybe, if he could get a good enough price, his grandmother would consider moving into the city, where Lion could keep an eye on her. "She's a little cantankerous with some people. I forgot about that."

"She loves you so much she would kill for you," Dorey whispered back. "So why should I be afraid of her?"

It was Violet who was suddenly uncomfortable in her own house. Dorey cleaned the kitchen floor without being asked, with a mixture of ash from the woodstove and a paste made from lye. This method left the old floorboards surprisingly clean, and the smell was oddly fresh, like mint or new cabbage. Dorey then went into the yard; she gathered the fallen pears, and, using the honey in the jar on the counter, and some chopped-up stale bread for a crust, she made something she called kuchen.

"I prefer it with plums," Dorey said. "But whoever gets plums in this lifetime? So I use whatever's nearby."

Violet had the need to be alone. To get away from this woman who knew how to deal with ashes, stones, bees, pears, lye, distrust. She went out to feed Bobby, then realized how cold it was. Cold enough for ice, at least at the edges of the pond. She hated the idea of electricity at the farm. Frankly, she wasn't really in favor of anything new. What was the future to her? Everything she loved had already happened and had already been. Violet hitched the little wagon she used to cart ice up to the old horse. It was getting harder to do so; her fingers hurt. And it took longer to guide Bobby over to the pond. It was nearly impossible to get him to stay put, even when he was roped to a tree, while she went to cut ice.

When Lion was a boy he could cut a whole wagonful of ice in little more than an hour. Every block was a different color, he'd say, if you only looked. Some ice was as green as emeralds, some of it was gray, like a dove, some chipped off in the pale, pale blue of morning, and other blocks, those from the very center of the pond, where the big catfish hid, were midnight.

Today just the shallows were frozen, but that was enough. Violet was glad for the work. She didn't want to think about her grandson in love. She didn't want to think about the way the birthmark on her face stung, only in sunlight when she was younger, and now a constant ache. By the time she chopped two square blocks, Violet's shoulders were strained. She looked back at the house and saw a plume of smoke rising from the chimney. Dorey had figured out the temperamental woodstove without any instructions; she hadn't had the least bit of trouble with it.

That's what Violet was thinking about when a big bird came soaring past, how some people knew how to deal with what happened to them in this world, and others did not. It was the white blackbird overhead that people saw occasionally on the property, an oddity that easily faded among the clouds. Violet herself wouldn't have been sure whether or not she'd actually seen it, but its call startled old Bobby, who'd been tied to a little sapling. One strong tug, and the fool horse was even more panicked, as the wagon bumped against him. He went running. He went blindly. He was onto the ice and into the water before Violet could even see what had happened.

Looking out the window, Dorey was thinking of the lake

where she and her sister used to skate. They used to hold hands, because her sister was younger and easily frightened and Dorey was not. They'd had a country house not unlike this one, and Dorey had loved to race through the fields. Back then, she believed that ice was made out of frozen teardrops and snow was made from broken hearts. She believed that she and her sister would always be safe, together in the house beside the lake. Now Dorey didn't think twice about running down to the pond. She didn't bother with shoes, because the soles of her feet were used to ice; she could will herself not to feel anything if need be. Certainly, she'd done it before.

The grandmother was up to her waist in the icy water, pulling on the wagon, screaming for Bobby. Dorey had heard people screaming for someone they loved many times before, not horses but children, not wagons but mothers and fathers, not those who could be saved but those who were already lost. She grabbed Violet West, who, though she was slight, had become heavy with icy water, pooling in her clothes and her shoes. The horse was gone; that was a fact. Dorey knew that it took less than two minutes to drown. No bubbles rising meant it was over already; there was no use going after the poor creature and going down as well, caught in the reins or trapped between the wheels of the cart. Dorey had considered drowning herself once; people often did it in a bucket. But she had heard it was a bad way to go—at the very last moment, the human constitution fought against drowning, and struggled to force the body to rise to the surface, even when it was impossible to survive.

Dorey pulled Violet West out of the pond where the ice turned so many colors Lion always said you could spend a lifetime trying to catalogue every shade. Both women were so cold they were gasping, open-mouthed, like fish. They were drenched, to the flesh, to the soul, and Dorey's feet were bluer than before, like the ice in the center of the pond, the midnight color Lion liked best.

"Okay?" Dorey asked the older woman.

Violet West nodded. Really, she wanted to cry. She thought about how stupid Bobby was, and how she loved him, and how she'd gotten so old in the blink of an eye, too old to stand without help from this woman who was sleeping with her grandson Lion, the one person on earth she would have traded her life for if need be.

"My father was a farmer, and he had a stubborn horse. I used to stand on a fence post and jump right onto his back." Dorey hadn't told Lion much about her family. She preferred to let him think she truly believed what was lost was gone forever.

"Is there anything you can't do?" Violet asked.

They had to hike up a hillock that didn't seem steep unless you were exhausted and freezing and barefoot.

"I can't have children," Dorey said.

There were icicles hanging from the pear tree, and from

the needles of the scrub pine, and from the roof of the house, which needed to be reshingled.

"They did that to me. I tried to tell Lion, but he doesn't want to listen. I can't change it, or make it different, or fix it. I can't wish it away. I can't will it away. He'll probably wind up hating me for it. And for everything else."

They got back to the house and took off all their clothes in front of the woodstove. Even with her failing vision, Violet West could see the scars. They had turned purple, almost red, from the icy cold, the color of the pears on the tree in the yard, the color of blood that can't be washed away and of things that can never be undone.

"He wants you to come and live with us." Dorey seemed perfectly at ease with no clothes on. Anything she had to hide was deep inside. "He told me last night. He's worried about you being on your own. What happened now will only make him more convinced he's right. You know Lion."

Violet West never expected to be standing in her own kitchen, naked, with a complete stranger. She never expected the ice would be so thin.

"What is it you want?" she said.

"I told you. I want to share him."

Dorey got dressed in some old clothes of Lion's—blue jeans, a white shirt—then she heated up the kuchen in a pan on top of the stove. She added a few extra spoonfuls of honey and some vanilla she found on a shelf. It was her mother's recipe that she used, one she'd memorized and repeated to herself night after night, the way some people repeat a lullaby or a charm. The kuchen was hot and ready to eat before Violet packed up the few belongings she had that still mattered to her. It was a simple dish, after all, and the two women were nearly finished when Lion walked through the door.

# THE WEDDING OF
# SNOW AND ICE

*I*N 1957, ON THE VERY RIM OF THE CAPE, a small town often didn't feel small until the first snowfall of the season. In those muffled first moments, in the hush and stillness before the flakes began and the anticipation of the mess there'd be to dig out afterward, people congregated in the general store, there to stock up on candles and flashlights, franks and beans, and loaves of bread. People regularly knew each other's business; now they could also recite what was in their neighbors' refrigerators and cupboards. Then and there, the world shrank and became a smaller thing, simple as a driveway, a red wicker basket filled with bread and milk, a cleared road, a light in a neighbor's window, a snow globe on a child's shelf.

At the Farrells', they were taking down the barn, and when the first big flakes began to fall, all work had to stop. There was no point in risking a slip on the roof and the possibility of a broken arm or leg. The Farrells, after all, were a cautious breed. The father, Jim, and the two boys, Hank and Jamie, trooped into the kitchen, their faces ruddy, hands frozen in spite of woolen gloves. Grace Farrell had been listening to the weather reports on the radio and had made tomato soup from the canned tomatoes left from last August's garden. The bowls of rich broth were so hot and delicious it made tears form in Jim's eyes, although, frankly, the boys preferred Campbell's.

Still, at fourteen and seventeen, the Farrell brothers knew enough to compliment their mother's soup. When they'd foolishly made their preference known in the past, their mother, mostly easygoing but with occasional frightening spikes of passion that surprised one and all, had spilled the entire contents of the pot down the drain. She, who liked things homemade and was known for her grape jam and Christmas pudding, announced she didn't know why she bothered with any of it. She might just get herself a job, and then where would they be? Eating bread and butter and soup right out of the can. She'd been a nurse when Jim Farrell met her, and she'd given it up to take care of them, and did they even appreciate what she'd sacrificed? Why, next summer she might even let the garden go wild if that was how little they thought of the work she put in. The garden was a trial anyway, a constant war against the naturalized sweet peas, vines so invasive Grace Farrell yanked them out by the handful. In the early fall, she'd had the older boy, Hank, hack down the vines with an ax, then build a bonfire. The smoke that arose was so sweet Grace Farrell wound up crying. She said there was smoke in her eyes, but she got like that sometimes, as if there was another life somewhere out there she might be living, one she might prefer despite her love for her husband and sons.

The sweet peas in the field were thought to have been set down by the first inhabitant of the house, Coral Hadley, who lost her husband and son at sea. Coral was said never to look at the ocean again after that, even though it was little more than a mile from her door. She dug in tightly to the earth, and there were people who vowed that her fingers turned green. When she walked down Main Street acorns fell out of her pockets, so that anyone following too closely behind was sure to stumble. Coral certainly did her best to cultivate this acreage. All these years later, her presence was still felt; odd, unexpected specimens popped up on the property, seeming to grow overnight. Peach trees where none belonged. Hedges of lilac of a variety extinct even in England. Roses among the nettle. The two-acre field rampant with those damned sweet peas, purple and pink and white, strong as weeds, impossible to get rid of.

Grace Farrell had stated publicly that she would swear old Coral Hadley came back from the dead just to replant anything that had been ripped up. Surely a joke, considering that Grace was one of the most sensible individuals around, the last woman you'd ever expect might believe in ghosts, the first a body could depend upon in times of trial and strife. She'd had her hands full with those boys of hers: Hank was the dreamer who didn't pay attention to his schoolwork. Jamie was the wilder one who simply couldn't sit still. In grammar school the fourth-grade teacher, Helen Morse, had tied Jamie's left arm to the desk in an attempt to force him to improve his penmanship by using his right hand, but Jamie had simply walked around the room dragging the desk along with him. He remained victorious, stubbornly left-handed.

He certainly had energy, that boy. He had to be kept busy, for his own good as well as for the peace of mind of those around him. Fortunately, they didn't have to think up projects. There were endless tasks around the house. The shaky old barn pulled down for safety's sake, for instance, though the boys had loved to play there when they were younger, swinging from a rope in the hayloft, nearly breaking their necks every time. New kitchen cabinets had just been put in, and Jamie had helped Jim with that job as well.

He'd been just as helpful when the dreadful stained car-
peting was at last taken up, exposing the yellow-pine floors
that were said to be soaked with Coral Hadley's tears.

There was always something gone wrong with a house
as old as this one. Maybe Grace should have said no when
Jim first took her to see the place. It was the week before
their wedding, and Grace was still living with her parents
up in Plymouth. She had recently given up her job at the
hospital. *Isn't it gorgeous?* he'd said of the farm. It looked like
one of those tumbledown places you saw in the news magazines, with hound dogs lazing around the front door. The
fields were so thick with milkweed back then that a thousand goldfinch came to feed every spring. Anyone wishing
to reach the pond had to use a scythe to cut a path. All the
same, the look on Jim's face had made Grace say, *Oh, yes.* It
had made her throw all good sense away. For an instant the
house did look beautiful to her, all white clapboards and
right angles; the milkweed was shining, illuminated by thin
bands of sunlight, an amazing sight if you looked at it the
right way, if you narrowed your eyes until everything
blurred into one bright and gleaming horizon.

Jim Farrell had grown up in town. His father had been
a carpenter, and Jim, wanting steadier work, was the chief
of the public-works department, the chief of three other
men, at any rate. He was a good man, quiet, not one to
shirk responsibility. People said he could smell snow, that
he could divine a nor'easter simply from the scent in the

air. The biggest storms smelled like vanilla, he'd confided to Jamie, the small ones like wet laundry. Tonight, Jim seemed antsy. He got like that when he simply couldn't tell what the snow was up to, when the whole damn thing seemed like a mystery. His job, after all, was a cat-and-mouse game against nature and fate. Did he get the town plows out early? Did he conserve sand and salt for the next snowfall? Would the storm carve away at the dunes, which were already disappearing all along the shore?

When Jim had finished his soup and taken his bowl to the sink, he stood at the window facing west. The field of sweet peas was already dusted white. Snow made him feel like crying sometimes—just the first flakes, the purest stuff.

Behind the hedge of holly the Brooks house next door was dark.

"Do you think I should go over there with some soup?" Grace had come up behind her husband. She liked the way he looked at snow, the intensity on his face, there when they made love, there whenever he was concentrating and trying to figure things out. "Hal might be away. I think he might still be working on that house in Bourne. She might be alone there with Josephine."

The Brookses were their closest neighbors, right there on the other side of the field, but there was no camaraderie between the families. Hal Brooks was a shit, there was no other way to say it, and even Grace, who was offended by bad language, would nod when someone in town referred to her neighbor that way. Lord, he'd been a mean snake all his life, the way Grace had heard it. Even as a boy, he'd shoot seagulls for sport, and once or twice a stray dog had disappeared on his property, only to be found strung up from one of the oak trees. Hal hadn't changed with age, and people in town all knew what was going on over there. You could see it when the Brookses' name came up. A nod. A stepping back. Some people had seen what went on with his wife, some had heard about it. The rest would simply cross the street when the Brookses were in town.

"If she needs something she'll come and get it, won't she?" Jim said, although they both thought this probably wasn't true.

The boys were in the living room watching the new TV; they would watch anything that flickered up in front of them, and for a while at least Jamie, always so restless, would settle down. The boys didn't need to know what went on at the Brookses'. When Grace and Jim had first moved in, Arly Brooks was the only occupant, a widower, a hardworking fisherman who kept his boat out in Provincetown. Hal had inherited the house from his father, and had come to claim it after the old man died. He'd arrived home from the Navy with this wife of his, ready to make enemies left and right no matter how many welcome baskets were

brought to the door or how many women in town sent
over pies. Jim Farrell didn't want his wife next door for any
reason, not even to take over a pot of soup.

"Stay away," Jim told Grace. "We all decide our own
fates, and what they do is their business."

"Well, of course I won't go over. But I might send the
boys to shovel snow."

Jim couldn't say no to that. Just last year, Mattie Ham-
mond, eighty-four years old and all on her own, had been
snowed into her cottage during a blizzard. The drifts had
been so high, Mattie couldn't open her front door and had
nearly starved to death before Jim came to plow out the
street. Despite the blanket of white that could cause semi-
blindness in some men while they were at the plow, Jim
had noticed the square handkerchief Mattie had taped up
in a window to signal her distress. There were some things
Jim Farrell couldn't deny a neighbor, particularly on a
snowy night, and other situations Grace couldn't turn away
from either, and because they didn't like to argue with each
other, no matter their differences, they left it at that.

Jim went out to his truck at four in the afternoon,
headed for the department of public works. It was the hour
when everything turned blue—the snow, the white fences,
the white clapboards of the house—that luminous time
when the line between earth and sky disappeared.

"I want you boys to go shovel over at Rosalyn Brooks',"
Grace called into the living room. She had ladled out a sep-

arate pot of tomato soup despite what Jim had advised. "Take the shovels and bring this soup with you."

When there was no response, Grace went into the living room and stood in front of the TV. The boys would watch just about anything, but their favorite show was *You Asked For It*, on tonight at seven. There were the most amazing things out there in the world, and all you had to do was ask and you'd see it right in front of you, on your very own screen.

"I'm turning this off," Grace announced, then did so. "I want you to shovel."

"At the Brookses'," Jamie said. "We heard."

"Can't. I've got a history paper," Hank said. "Sorry, Mom, but it's due tomorrow."

Hank was having his troubles in school, so Grace let him stay and sent Jamie on his own, making sure he bundled up, handing him his hat, which he often managed to forget, watching to make certain he pulled on his scarf and his leather gloves. The pot of soup was under one arm, the shovel carried over his shoulder. He was a quiet boy, not much of a student, but lovable to his mother in some deep way, so that she worried about him as she didn't anyone else in this world. Perhaps it was true that mothers had favorites, at least now and then. Grace watched Jamie disappear into the blue of the field and felt a catch in her throat. Love, she presumed. A moment of realizing exactly how lucky she was, of being grateful that she was not Coral

Hadley, that her son was not out on the ocean, but was instead traipsing through the snowy reaches of their own familiar acreage.

When he was alone, Jamie tended to hum. His mother was a fan of musicals, particularly *The King and I*, and Jamie found himself humming "Getting to Know You." His mother loved Yul Brynner, for reasons Jamie couldn't understand. The king he played was bald, for one thing; he was bossy as all get-out for another. All the same, the song stuck. Sometimes when Jamie walked through this field, in winter, at exactly this hour, he would see deer. There were wild turkeys too, crazy birds that had very little fear of humans and would run straight at you if you invaded their territory. There was a shortcut to the Brookses', through the winterberry vines. The berries were shiny and red; sometimes you'd happen upon a skunk as you made your way through the brambles, and that skunk would just go on feeding, calm as could be, rightfully assured that few creatures other than the neighborhood dogs would be stupid enough to interrupt or attack.

Jamie was in the winterberry, thinking about deer, singing softly to himself, when he heard it. A clap of thunder. A snowplow on the road. A firecracker. He stopped for a minute and breathed in snowflakes. When he breathed out, his breath was like a steam engine. It melted the snow off the winterberries. He listened. He was good at that, but he heard nothing, so he went on. He was that sort of boy, intent on the task at hand. He knew what his mother wanted him to do: shovel from the Brookses' front door to their driveway. He and Hank had done it before, last year. Mr. Brooks hadn't been at home, but Mrs. Brooks had made them hot chocolate, which they drank out on the front step. Now, alongside the Chevy, there was Mr. Brooks' truck, a wreck of a thing, battered, leaking oil into the snow.

Jamie tried to balance the soup on the front step, but the step was made from an uneven piece of stone. He went up to the door then, to deliver the soup before he started to work. His breath did the same thing to the glass window set into the door as it did to the winterberries, melted off the snow, then fogged it up. But even through the fog he could see Rosalyn Brooks, right there on the floor with no clothes on and something red all over her face. He should have backed away; he should have run home, done something, anything, but he had never seen a naked woman before, and it was as though he were hypnotized, frozen in place, while his breath kept melting the snow. One minute he had been a fourteen-year-old boy with nothing much on his mind. Now he was someone else entirely.

He was still holding on to the pot of tomato soup when he opened the door. People didn't lock up much in their town; there was nothing to steal and no one to steal it. Jamie walked in as though he'd been drawn inside by a magnetic force. The Brookses' house was an old farmhouse, like the Farrells', but it hadn't been updated. It was cold and empty, and the only light turned on was in the kitchen, all the way down the hall. Everything looked blue inside the house, except for the thing that was red. It was blood that was all over Rosalyn Brooks, but when she looked up and saw Jamie she seemed most panicked by the fact that she was naked. She let out a strange sound and grabbed for a rag rug, trying to cover herself. It was a sob, that's what Jamie realized. That was the sound.

"I brought you soup," he said. "It's from my mother."

Mrs. Brooks looked at him as though he were crazy.

"She makes it herself." Jamie felt like running, but he didn't seem capable of turning away. He had the feeling he might be paralyzed. "Are you all right?"

Rosalyn Brooks laughed, or at least Jamie thought that's what it was.

"Just stay there," he said. "I'll get you something."

He put the soup on a tabletop and went to the hall closet, grabbing for the first thing he felt, bringing back a heavy black woolen coat.

"It's okay," he said, because of the way she was looking at him. As though she was scared. "It's a coat."

Rosalyn Brooks stared at him, then took the coat and put it on. Jamie Farrell looked away; all the same, he glimpsed her breasts, blue in the light of the house, and her belly, which was oddly beautiful. She had bruises all over, that much he noticed as well, on her legs and shoulders especially. He saw now that her lip was split open and she could barely see through the slits of her eyes.

"Do you want me to heat you some soup?" It was so cold in the house that Jamie's breath came out in billows, and he was embarrassed by his own heat. When Mrs. Brooks didn't answer, he figured she wanted him to take the pot into the kitchen, but as he turned to head down the hall, Rosalyn lurched from her prone position and grabbed his pants leg. She did it so hard and so fast he almost fell over. She looked at him then in a way that convinced him something really bad had happened. Somebody else might have taken off running, back through the winterberries, snagging his clothes as he raced through the bushes, but Jamie crouched down beside Mrs. Brooks.

"Where's Josephine?" he asked.

That was the Brookses' little daughter. Josephine liked to pick the sweet peas in the field. She liked the pears that dropped to the ground from the big tree in the Farrells' yard. Rosalyn looked up the stairs.

"Is she in bed?"

"Asleep."

At least Mrs. Brooks could talk. That was a relief.

"My husband had an accident."

"Okay," Jamie said. "Should we call my dad? He could help."

"No. You can't call him."

He could tell that whatever had happened was bad from

her tone. Still, he stayed. Maybe Jamie felt he owed Rosalyn Brooks his allegiance because he'd seen her naked, or
maybe it was all that blood, or the way his breath was so
hot and the house so very cold.

"In the kitchen?"

Mrs. Brooks nodded. She was not yet thirty, a young
woman, pretty under other circumstances.

"I'll just go in there and get a dish towel to stop the
bleeding," Jamie said, for her lip and her scalp were oozing.

But when he rose, she grabbed his leg again.

"It's okay," he assured her. "I'll be right back."

The hallway was even colder. These old houses had no
insulation, and the kitchen was especially chilly. There was
even more blood on the floor, especially around Hal
Brooks' body, which was right in front of the stove. Jamie
tried not to look too closely. He grabbed a dish towel, ran
cold water over it, then brought it back to Rosalyn. He
wondered if he had stepped in the blood and if it was on
the soles of his boots, if he'd left tracks down the hall. Then
he stopped wondering. He put those thoughts aside. Rosalyn was sitting on the floor now, the coat buttoned; when
he handed her the dish towel, she held it up to her lip.

"What do you want to do with him?" Jamie said.

Outside, the blue was turning into darkness. A black
night. So quiet you could hear the cardinals nesting in the
hedges outside the Brookses' window. The snow fell

harder. Jamie figured his father was up on the main road with his plow by now.

They sat there in silence in the cold house.

"I'll shovel your path, and then I'll come back," Jamie said. "You think about what you want to do."

"Okay," Rosalyn said. "I will."

Jamie went out and shoveled hard and fast. It was heavy snow, thick and dense, the kind that he would have thought was good for snowball fights on any other occasion. He wasn't thinking that way now. He was thinking of the pond beyond the field. In the old days, food could be stored in the summer kitchen right up until July if enough ice was stacked against the walls. He'd heard the old woman who'd lived in their house a while back had hauled blocks of ice from the pond until her horse, the one who'd lived in the barn they'd begun to tear down, slipped through the ice and drowned.

The kitchen floor at the Brookses' was already clean when Jamie came back inside. Rosalyn Brooks had mopped up, then washed her face and pulled back her honey-colored hair. There were still streaks of blood in her scalp, but Jamie Farrell didn't have the heart to tell her. Rosalyn went to check on her daughter, then she came back down-stairs and put on her husband's workboots. She looked even more delicate wearing them. She didn't bother with gloves. At least there was a blanket around Mr. Brooks, and

Jamie was grateful for that. They tried to pull him along the floor, and when that didn't work, Jamie went and got the wheelbarrow from the garage. He was so hot he felt like taking off his hat and his scarf, but if he misplaced them, his mother would have his head.

It took all their combined strength to push the wheelbarrow through the snow. The thick, heavy snow that they quietly cursed. They stopped for a break halfway across the field; they both looked up at the falling snow. Rosalyn put her arms out, and tilted her head back. Jamie had never thought about the future, who he was, what he would do. It had all been a haze. Now he saw that blood was still seeping through Rosalyn's hair and he thought she probably needed stitches. He saw that his future was almost here.

There were pine trees and holly around the far side of the pond, and that's where they went. They had to drag him along over the frozen weeds. They put stones in his pockets, heavy black stones, the kind Jamie and Hank liked best for their slingshots. Rosalyn took off the workboots she'd been wearing and filled them with stones as well, then put the boots on her husband, laced them and carefully tied a knot, then a double-knot.

"Your feet will freeze on the way back," Jamie whispered.

She didn't seem to care. She closed her eyes, and when she opened them they were still slits. The snow was making things quieter all the time. They pulled him into the

pond and watched him sink. There was a gulping noise at
first, then there was nothing. Only the quiet.

"You go home," Rosalyn said to Jamie. "Go on. Your
mother will be worried."

He hated to leave her like that, barefoot, bleeding.

She leaned over and kissed him, on the lips, in gratitude.

Jamie Farrell ran the rest of the way, his hot breath rattling against his ribs. His boots and pants legs were wet and
mucky. There was pond water in his boots, fetid, cold stuff.
He was shivering and couldn't stop. Worst of all, his
mother was waiting for him.

"What took you so long?" Grace demanded. "It's after
eight. You missed your TV show." Then, looking at him
carefully, "Where's the shovel?"

"I forgot it." Jamie turned back to the door. "I'm sorry.
I'll go get it if you want."

His mother stopped him. She looked at him harder still.
"I'll go. You do your homework and get ready for bed."

"I can get the shovel in the morning," Jamie offered, an
edge of panic inside him. But Grace was already getting her
coat. She had stepped into her warm black boots. After she
left, Jamie went up to the bedroom he shared with his
brother. It was as though he'd just walked out of a dream
and here he was, melting in the overheated second floor of
his family's house. He thought of all the wounded people
there were in this world, people he'd never even know, and
he felt helpless.

"What if I was an accessory to murder?" he asked Hank, who was already in bed, more than half asleep as he gazed at his history book.

"What if you were the biggest moron that ever lived?" Hank shot back, a question for which there was no answer, at least not on this night.

It was nearly midnight by the time Grace came home. The snow was tapering off, and she brushed the flakes from her coat and stomped on the welcome mat to dislodge the ice from her boots. Usually, Jim didn't get back till dawn, but tonight he'd come home earlier. The storm wasn't as bad as the meteorologists had predicted. His men could take care of the rest of the cleanup.

"Where were you? The boys are in bed, and when you weren't here, I didn't know what to think."

But that wasn't true. For a moment, what he'd thought was that she'd left him. Just disappeared into that other life she seemed to be thinking about sometimes. They stared at each other now, their breath hot. Outside, the drifts leaned against the house; winter here stayed a long time.

"I went over and heated up the tomato soup for Rosalyn."

"Did you?"

Grace sat down at the table. Everyone had known what was going on, and no one had done a damn thing about it.

"Hal up and left. No money, no warning, nothing. She thinks he may have re-enlisted."

Jim was looking out the window; two deer had just now wandered into their field. He hoped the snow wasn't deep enough to prevent them from unearthing the last withered sweet peas, thought to be delicious by anything wild. "I guess it's none of our business," he said. From this distance, the winterberries almost looked tropical, the fruit of another place entirely.

"So you say."

Grace Farrell still had snow in her hair, but it would melt when they got into bed, and she'd never even know it had been there. When she thought back to this night, she wouldn't even remember it had been snowing, she'd only remember the look on her husband's face, the concentration she loved, the man she could turn to, even on a night as cold as this.

# INDIA

M Y MOTHER TOLD ME THAT THE BLACK-
birds were singing on the day they found the
house. You could hear them from the road.
It was a wave of sound, black and blue and
sweet. Like a bruise that was healing, nothing but peace and harmony. That was how
my parents knew they had reached their
destination. It was a November day at the
very end of nineteen sixty-nine; the earth
and sky were gray, and my parents were at
the very tip of the world, or so it seemed.

My father had been born John Adams-
Cooper, but he called himself Risha, which
was Hindu for those whose birthdays fall

under the sign of the bull. When we were teenagers, my brother and I used to say it was actually the sign for bull-shit. All the same, my father had a dumb-animal accept-ance of things, good or bad, and if that made him a bull, so be it. He had studied with a yogi in Cambridge, but was still suffering from exhaustion and post-traumatic stress. He had decided that cities were bad for humanity, so my parents had taken to the road and kept moving, from Ver-mont, to New Hampshire, to the far reaches of the Cape, where at last those blackbirds stopped them cold. It was an omen, my mother was certain of it. Twenty-four blackbirds in a row on the roof of the house, one for every hour of every day. One of the birds appeared to be white, and surely that must be a sign of good fortune to come. My fa-ther had just inherited some money from the aunt who'd raised him, an unexpected windfall. The house was destiny, my mother told me; the path that was meant to be.

Of course, anyone with the least bit of sense would have been instantly aware that this ramshackle farm was no one's shining path. It had been on the market for five years, the family house of the doctor in town, sold when he moved his family to a larger place in the village. It appealed to none of the locals. People said it was haunted. Boys threw stones at the windows; girls vowed that if you had the nerve to walk past the big old pear tree, then turn around twice, the man you were destined to marry would appear on the road.

The place was a wreck, that much was certain, not that my parents noticed. The heater had been torn out. The roof was leaking. The plumbing ceased to function whenever the temperature went below freezing, so that the outhouse was still utilized, even though you could freeze your bum in a matter of minutes. All the same, no one could dissuade my mother, who had once been Naomi Shapiro of Great Neck, Long Island, but who had become someone else completely. She was a woman who saw what she wanted to see: Therefore, it was love that had drawn them to the house where my brother and I grew up. It was fortune, perfection, nothing less than bliss.

My mother often got things backward; I knew that early on. She made irrevocable mistakes, such as going to Boston one weekend when she was a nineteen-year-old sophomore at Vassar and meeting my father on the Common and falling in love when it was the last thing in the world she should have done. It was crazy, the act of a foolish, impressionable girl. If Naomi had really understood omens she would have recognized these signs: My father was thirty-five when she met him, far too old for her, much too damaged. He'd served in Vietnam and hadn't held a job since his return to Massachusetts. Was this her destiny? Naomi Shapiro read tarot cards. Did she not see exactly what the future would bring?

All the same, my father had a beautiful face, with strong features my mother mistook for inner strength. She didn't know until they spent the night together that he cried himself to sleep. He had such terrible nightmares that he ground his teeth until the enamel cracked. But after that first night, embracing each other on the floor of an apartment belonging to someone they barely knew, it was probably too late to walk away. The more wounded my father was, the more tightly my mother was tied to him. If she'd been wiser or older or simply more experienced, she would have known that any man who professes his love for you half an hour after he meets you is a man who has his feet planted squarely in his dreams. In my father's case, all of those dreams were nightmares, nothing anyone should be destined to share, no future to wish for, no destiny to desire.

My mother was also mistaken about those blackbirds that were perched along the roof of our house. They were bad luck, not good. Everyone knows a white blackbird is nothing more than a ghost, a shadow of what it ought to be. And that line of birds didn't signify twenty-four hours, but twenty-four years, for that was how long my parents were married. My brother, Kalkin, and I, one year apart, were both born in the summer kitchen, a shed with a dirt floor at the rear of the property. My parents didn't believe in hospitals; they believed in meditation and in the natural order of things. My father had remained a devotee of the Maharishi and of Krishna consciousness; therefore, simplicity was the path. My father was convinced that babies in India came into this world easily, while the mothers focused on a single bead of sweat; too much fuss was made here in the U.S. But my brother, Kalkin, was always difficult; even before he was born, he didn't abide by my father's plans. Kalkin had to be turned and persuaded to leave the womb. Fortunately, our neighbor, Josephine Brooks, came to check in on my mother, and Miss Brooks ran back to her house to phone Dr. Farrell. The doctor, having grown up in this same house, was most likely shocked by its current state when he came to deliver my brother, after Kal refused to be born naturally. Dr. Farrell returned the following year, for safety's sake, surely as an afterthought, for me.

For years Kal and I went to the shed, stunned that we'd been born there. Was it possible, in this day and age? Was it even legal to do such a thing? We watched TV at Nancy Lanahan's house whenever we had the chance. We knew children were supposed to be born in clean hospital rooms with nurses hovering over the laboring mothers and medical equipment available in case of emergency. We knew our parents were not like other people. Every day, in every way, they proved this to us. We had simple longings, Kalkin and I, for store-bought white bread, for ironed clothes and boxes of chocolates, the kind my mother said would rot a person's teeth and make him hyperactive.

My father had no job; his idea of work was to cut down the tall grass in our field at the end of the summer, then store the hay in the shed where we'd been born. My mother now kept two sheep there, for their wool. She supported us with her weavings—intricate, beautiful things—but it wasn't enough. We were poor, although that wasn't the problem: it was how prideful our parents were about our lowly circumstances, as though our lack of possessions made us better somehow. We were superior beings because we used the woodstove to heat the downstairs in winter, and piled up blankets on our beds so we wouldn't freeze during the night. We ate rice and beans at the end of every month. We wore our clothes until they all but disintegrated, and even then my mother, who had grown up with a closet full of clothes I would have coveted, cashmere and leather and lace, sewed gingham patches on our jeans, which my brother ripped off the minute he left the house.

*Fuck this*, he would say. Kalkin seemed harder with every year, as though he had a shell around him, one nothing could penetrate. The cold no longer affected him. He never wore a winter coat. He refused to bother with a hat or an umbrella. He was invincible, that was Kalkin, and he would manage to outwit our parents someday. The holes in his clothes only clarified matters—he was too good for the life we were living. He had been misplaced somehow, left on a doorstep, born in a shed, meant for another world entirely.

We were supposedly vegetarians, but Kalkin and I wolfed down hamburgers and beef stew at our friend

Nancy Lanahan's house whenever we were lucky enough to be invited to dinner. The Lanahans' place was a modest ranch half a mile down our street, but to us it was perfect. There was a telephone, a television, two parents who worked, food in the refrigerator, what more could anyone ask for? We would have moved into Nancy's house if given half the chance. We hated our farm, our parents, our lives. We especially hated our sheep, Padma and Brownie, who were terribly stupid. They ate my mother's garden, got trapped in the nettle, were often stuck in the mud at the shore of the pond. The sheep panicked whenever Kal and I crept up on them, bolting as though we were wolves rather than children. It was somehow thrilling to chase those silly creatures through the meadow shouting *Lamb chops!*, racing through the milkweed until we thought our hearts would burst and we felt flushed with a vague sense of embarrassment. It wasn't the lambs who were our enemies; why take it out on them?

One winter, when Kal was sixteen and I fifteen, he made a vow that he would move away to Los Angeles. It was December, a clear, starry night, and we were walking home from Nancy's house. The snow crunched under our boots; the air was so salty and cold every breath we took hurt. By then, Nancy was in love with my brother. Although Nancy swore they had almost gone all the way while I was busy watching *Dallas* on the family's TV and they were hidden beneath a quilt, Kal was not about to be tied down. When he made his vow to leave home, I felt like crying. I knew he would keep his promise. He was like that, strong in the face of weakness, as reliable as he was unforgiving. It was almost as though he were already gone when he was right there beside me, walking down the road, our collars turned up, our jeans so worn the wind cut right through the fabric.

Most of the kids in town knew that our father was growing marijuana in the field beyond our house, that he smoked it daily before he went out to meditate in the summer kitchen or down near the shoreline, where the tall reeds grew. They thought it was funny, an old man still at it. They thought we were lucky not to have rules and regulations, not even any expectations, it seemed. Now we could hear our father chanting down at the pond. I wished my parents knew I preferred those rich, snotty people on *Dallas* to them. I ached to be living at South Fork right then and there, my hair dyed blond and poufed way out, diamond rings on every one of my fingers.

"Fucking idiot," my brother said of Risha on that cold night. "I cannot be genetically related to him. I'm getting out of here, Maya. If you're smart, you will, too."

My brother had inherited my father's jawline, from the Adams-Cooper side of the family. He was beautiful, but he didn't know it, with golden hair that turned nearly white in the summers. I had my mother's curly dark hair, my father's gray eyes, and nothing else that belonged to them.

Unlike most of the kids we knew, my brother and I didn't smoke pot or get into trouble at school. We disdained those who did. My brother especially wanted to prove his heredity was a mistake; therefore, fun was out of the question. Foolish actions unthinkable. I was more cautious. Why should I work hard when I wasn't certain we would ever escape our parents' legacy? I let my brother be the guinea pig, waiting to see if he could right all that was wrong in our lives. He worked at the gas station, sold Christmas trees culled from our property, and later on, when he was a senior in high school, started selling our father's homegrown. He earned enough of a profit to allow him to move to Los Angeles two weeks after high-school graduation.

Kal had probably earned more money by the age of eighteen than my father had in his entire lifetime, but he had bigger dreams. He wasn't about to stay in our little town, where the tides were the biggest topic of conversation down at the general store, and a storm was huge news to one and all. Nancy tried her best to make my brother stay. She arrived on our doorstep on the night before he went away, weeping, hair in tangles, professing her love. When Kal told her they were through, she cut her wrists in our driveway, but even that wasn't enough to make Kalkin stay. He calmly poured a pot of water on the spot, to wash the blood away, so the coyotes wouldn't gather there at dusk.

"I must have done something wrong," my mother said about Kal turning so hard. He wouldn't even let them drive him to the airport; he took the bus instead.

"Everyone has his own path," my father said. His hair was so long he had to braid it to keep it out of his eyes. All at once, it had turned gray. Risha wasn't that much older than my friends' parents, but he seemed ancient.

I laughed at my father's vision of the world. I really did. For as long as I could remember, he had been planning a trip to India. One of his old army buddies who had come for dinner said he'd been dreaming about this journey even back when they were enlisted men. But so far, my father's path had led only to the field behind our house. As for my mother, it was too late for her to actualize her maternal instincts. She had cried for days when her lamb Padma died, but when I had scarlet fever I had to walk down the road to Nancy's and call the doctor myself. If I'd left my fate in my mother's hands I could have died, just to prove the point that medicine was overused.

"You've done quite a bit wrong," I informed my mother. "Try everything."

She was selfish and silly, and now she wasn't even pretty anymore. She should have stayed Naomi Shapiro and led a normal life instead of weeping over lambs and watching her only son pack up and flee the moment he could. She should have once suggested that I brush my hair.

Risha hardly seemed to notice Kalkin's departure. He

was busy with another one of his projects that he never completed. That summer when my brother left for Los Angeles, my father was involved in taking our kitchen apart. He had milled some beautiful applewood for the floors, and the house smelled like cider, a sad odor that got into our clothes and our hair. No one used applewood for a floor, it was among the most delicate of woods, sure to scratch and be damaged, but my father didn't care about such matters. Not Risha, the bull. He'd set up a grill in the summer kitchen, that shack where Kal and I had been born, so my mother could cook out there. We still had Brownie, the dark sheep, but Brownie was old and feeble and followed my mother around, crying when she wasn't let into the house or the summer kitchen. Brownie sounded like a human being sometimes; then I'd catch sight of her, standing like a stone in the farthest field, searching out my mother in the exact wrong direction, and my compassion would fade. I had become stony myself now that my brother was gone. It had always been two against two: The two of us normal, outraged, horrified. The two of them burning Mumtaz incense, chanting late at night so that sometimes I'd wake from a sound sleep and imagine I was in a foreign country, one from which there was no escape.

My brother got a job with a movie producer, and that didn't surprise me. Everyone wanted a piece of Kalkin. He was so golden, so sure of himself, a genetic wonder. Nancy

Lanahan quickly gained twenty pounds pining for him. She wrote strange verse on her skin with a ballpoint pen, and her parents became so distressed they took her up to Boston on Saturdays to see a psychiatrist. Nancy had pretty much stopped talking to me. For some reason she blamed me for not stopping my brother from fleeing Massachusetts, as if I could convince him of anything. Our relationship didn't work that way. Kalkin did as he pleased, and I meekly followed. Sometimes I stood with that stupid Brownie in the field and thought I probably felt the same way she did without Padma. A creature without direction, spooked by the wind in the milkweed, by the thud of apples as they fell from the trees.

Loneliness is a bad thing most times. Worse when you're seventeen. It can become nasty and hopeless, and that's what happened to me. I stopped talking to my father, not that we'd ever had much to say. I'd see him working on rebuilding the kitchen and I'd just know it would take a full year or more for him to finish. I could feel my bitterness rising. In the winter Naomi would still be traipsing out to the summer kitchen to start a fire in the grill. The most ridiculous thing was, she wouldn't even complain. I wanted to shake my mother and say: *Wake up! This is the man you married, smoking pot out in the woods, making certain every plank in the kitchen floor is perfectly planed while the rest of the house falls down around us and Kalkin is three thousand miles away. What have you done to yourself? To us? To our lives?*

I kept thinking about the day my mother told me about, when they first found this house. That day felt like a curse, like the cold hand of fate. So I started to try and figure out who these people were, these strangers, my parents. I took the train to New York, then went on to the Long Island Railroad in order to meet my mother's older sister, Judith, at a Chinese restaurant in Great Neck. My aunt looked like my mother, only reflected in a fun mirror at a carnival. She was both like Naomi and completely different. Whereas my mother cultivated her plainness, Judith was wearing diamonds and had on a chic black suit I coveted the minute I saw it. Actually, she reminded me of Sue Ellen from *Dallas*, only not quite so sympathetic.

My aunt took one peek at me and was clearly disappointed. I looked like I was from the sticks, I knew that. A bedraggled long-lost niece. I was no prize, I understood that much. All the same, we had lunch, and I prayed my aunt would pick up the check. Judith told me about her daughters, my cousins, one at Smith and the other at Brown. *Well, la-di-da,* I almost said, but I kept my mouth shut. She told me about her husband's desire to move into Manhattan now that the girls were gone, even though co-ops were so expensive. I really didn't care. I wanted to know about Naomi. When I asked what had happened to my mother, why was she so different, my aunt couldn't tell me much. Judith had been five years older and obviously self-absorbed; she'd never paid much attention to little

Naomi, who was bookish and sweet, nobody's problem. Then that sweet little girl went and married that lunatic, and that was the end of her as far as the family was concerned. Why she had done so was anyone's guess.

"She always did have a bleeding heart," my aunt informed me as I was leaving. "That kind of thing can get you in trouble if you don't watch out."

I thought about that remark on the way home. Naomi's heart bled for my father, it was true; you could see that by the way she cared for him. She drove fifty miles in order to buy the green tea he preferred. She waited up for him and prided herself on never having gone to bed without him. After I returned from New York, whenever I looked at Naomi, I saw her bleeding heart and I felt my coldness for my father in the pit of my stomach. My bitterness was turning to poison. My father had ruined all our lives for no particular reason. Just vanity, nothing more. We'd never had much to say to each other, now there was nothing. We had no telephone, so when I wanted to call Kal I had to go over to Miss Brooks' house next door and use the phone in her kitchen. Miss Brooks worked at the library in town and was used to whispers; she was graceful enough to pretend not to hear me when I begged Kal to come home. Sometimes when I did this I cried. I could tell Kal was getting impatient with me. He had his life in Los Angeles. He had been promoted, gotten a larger apartment, after only six months. There were women who would have done anything for him; men who wished their own sons had as much drive and ambition as Kal. It was his world, his dream, his reality, his life.

"I told you, leave," my brother said. "Get your grades up. Apply to college. Just get out of there."

From my neighbor's window I could see Brownie standing in our field.

"Thanks," I said to Kalkin. I was a sour apple. I was a bitter pill. "Many, many thanks for all your consideration. You're just as selfish as they are."

My father with India, Kalkin with Los Angeles, what was the difference? It was all about them. Their lives. Their dreams.

My brother was killed on the 105 Freeway two weeks after we spoke. He'd bought a Mustang covertible. It was dusk and he was driving carefully, which figured, but that wasn't enough. Someone two lanes over was drunk, and that was the end of my brother. We didn't even know until the next day. No one could call us; we didn't have a phone. Josephine Brooks came over after she got the call from a friend of Kal's in L.A. Miss Brooks was wearing all black, and she looked like a cloud moving across the sky. She knocked at our door, even though it was never latched. Everyone knew my parents didn't believe in locks and keys.

When I saw the look on my mother's face I knew what had happened. I knew right away that we had somehow managed to lose him. My heart broke, then and there.

I didn't wait for my father, who was out in the summer kitchen, repairing the roof with old newspapers and tar. I ran over to Nancy Lanahan's and I threw myself into Mrs. Lanahan's arms. My brother was the only person I had loved in this world. I never got to tell him, but I think he knew. All the same, my love was like an anchor, too heavy to bear. He was probably running away from me, too. I stayed at the Lanahans' house all that week. Nancy took pity on me, forgave me my earlier trespasses, and cried right along with me. She stopped eating and lost all that weight she'd gained when my brother moved away. I guess her parents were used to girls who had nervous break-downs, who were easily unwound by grief. They even took me to see Nancy's psychiatrist once, but the doctor had nothing worthwhile to offer me. In time, grief dissipates. That's all he told me. What did that mean? Did it disap-pear, like a cloud, or did it rain down and saturate every-thing, every minute, every day, every detail in your life? It wasn't a good enough answer. I couldn't stop thinking Kalkin's name. If I had told my father that, he would tell me some nonsense about how Kal's name was now my mantra, my personal path to enlightenment.

Risha actually came looking for me at the end of the week. He seemed even more ridiculous than usual standing in the Lanahans' living room. Risha was tall and he had to crouch. He blinked in the light. The TV was on, and my father seemed distracted by its wavering picture. He'd been in battle, my mother had once let that slip; he'd had to do terrible things. But I couldn't imagine Risha killing anyone. I couldn't imagine him moving through the real world, not then and not now. When he spoke to the Lanahans, he repeated himself; he seemed foggy, and he blew his nose on an old handkerchief. Even his voice didn't sound the same. Not to my ears. Nancy's father shook Risha's hand and told him he was sorry to hear about my brother, a boy who had so much promise. My father looked confused. He made a weird sound in his throat.

I was lying on the floor, on the nice wool carpet, gold, like a field of mustard. I turned my head away. If I pretended I was asleep, maybe my father would believe it. He was easily convinced of things. He'd always told Kalkin and me that he had seen the ghost of a sailor in the woods on several occasions. *I'll bet he does,* Kal had laughed. *If I smoked as much pot as he did, I'd be seeing that sailor, too.* But in fact Josephine Brooks had told me the very same thing. There had indeed been a sailor who had built our house, she'd said, and he'd been lost at sea.

How fitting, I'd thought. My father was equally lost. He had dropped through a hole in the universe at some point, and had been dragging us along with him ever since. Now he was standing in the Lanahans' living room, still wanting to pull me down. I thought about drowning and what that might feel like. I thought of the color blue and the rush of the cold tide, of arms and legs that were paralyzed by the sheer weight of the water. So I pretended I was asleep. Mrs. Lanahan promised to tell me that my father had come for me. She would relay the message that my mother was worried. I had already missed the service they'd had for my brother out in the woods, where they'd sprinkled his ashes, sent from Los Angeles, with us now forevermore. That was something I couldn't forgive; I would have saved some of his remains in a pouch I kept with me at all times. I would have carried him away from here.

I think the Lanahans knew that night that I wasn't leaving. They were kind, decent people; perhaps their hearts bled for me as well. I was pathetic, I suppose, but I made certain to be useful around the house, cleaning the kitchen, shoveling snow, praying they wouldn't see me for who I really was and ask me to leave. I stayed until the end of that year, until graduation. I counted to a hundred whenever I passed by the farm. I didn't look at the house or the field. I could no longer tell the difference between my father chanting and the sound of the wind. Soon enough, Nancy fell in love with her bio lab partner, but I didn't hope for anything like love. I got good grades instead, and, following Kal's suggestion, I applied to Columbia, where I was given a scholarship.

I went home once, to inform my parents that I would be moving to New York. No one had told me, but Brownie had died in my absence. The field looked empty, even though it was late spring and the wild sweet peas were rampant. When you stood in the driveway all you saw was green and purple. There was a haze over everything, as though this were already the past. I thought about my brother and how all he'd wanted was to get away and now he was here forever. I thought about hearts that bled and my mother when she was a girl in New York, standing in front of her closet, not seeing anything that was worthwhile.

My parents already knew about my scholarship. There had been a notice in the local paper, along with a photograph, so my mother wasn't surprised that I'd cut my hair. No one was wearing wild, long hair anymore, except for my parents. My mother hugged me at the door, and I admit that I stood there, frozen for a moment, before I came in for a cup of tea. My father had finished the floor, and our woodstove had been reinstalled, but the plumbing was worse than ever. My mother had to carry buckets from the pond and boil the mucky water on the woodstove. The tea she made for us tasted like mint and silt. It was undrinkable. As for my father, he was nowhere to be seen. I thought he was probably avoiding me, but that didn't matter. *Don't tell me he finally got off his ass and went to India,* I said. It was supposed to be a joke, but my mother slapped me. I lurched backward, stunned. My mother didn't believe in corporal punishment, or in discipline, or even in anger.

*Don't you dare disrespect your father*, she said. She, who wept at the death of lambs, who didn't partake of the modern world, who'd never been anything or anyone I wanted her to be. *You have no idea of who your father is, or what he went through. Don't think you have the right to judge him.*

We were done with each other, that much was clear. We were total strangers and had been all along. I didn't understand Risha, and I certainly didn't understand my mother. What on earth could have made her stay with him for so long? Even a heart as big and foolish as hers couldn't bleed for this long, could it? I had planned to go up to my room, but I didn't want anything that had belonged to me when I lived here. I smelled apples from the wood floor. I took the bus to Boston, then got on the train. It was easy. You just paid your money and they gave you a ticket. It was so easy, it almost felt wrong.

In spite of the way I left, something from home stayed with me. Sometimes in New York City I'd smell apples. An olfactory hallucination, imaginary, but disconcerting all the same. I'd see homeless men on the street and think they were my father, come to track me down. He never did. He didn't believe in things like that. He believed every person had his own path, and that it was our journey in this lifetime to discover the meaning of our own destiny.

My father was out in the field where he had scattered my brother's ashes when he died. He liked to be with my brother, my mother told me later; he missed Kalkin terribly. He cried worse than ever at night. My father was only sixty, too young to be so ill, but my mother told me he did not fear death, not even at the end. It was cancer and he hadn't a chance, but every day he sat in the field and watched the sun rise. He still didn't believe in hospitals, and in his case it wouldn't have helped. So he waited. He sat in one place for so long the goldfinches took him for a stone and perched on his shoulders. The cold did not bother him, nor did his pain. He swore he saw the sailor who had built our house, the one who had disappeared out on the ocean. There were waves in the field where Padma and Brownie had lived, and my father could smell the sea, only a mile away. He counted blackbirds until they became stars to his eyes. He said my name was the most beautiful word in the universe, and that was why he had called me Maya, but I had never really heard the word.

After my mother told me these things, I went out past the summer kitchen, where my brother and I had been born. I'd worked during my summers in New York, and I had enough saved to take my father to India. I could buy the plane tickets tomorrow on my credit card, for myself and my mother. We could have brought his ashes there. But my mother had laughed at that suggestion. India was just something he talked about. My mother had already spread my father's ashes in the field where the sweet peas and milkweed grew. She did it even though her heart bled for him; she held up whole handfuls of bone one windy day, her love given up to the universe, her gratitude outweighing her sorrow.

Standing in that field, I realized that I was lost, and that my path, if I had one, was completely unknown to me. The house looked small, so tiny I might have held it in the palm of my hand. I had gone in a circle, trying to escape myself. There were the sweet peas that had bloomed in my childhood. There was the milkweed that drifted into the sky whenever the wind came in from the sea. I said the word "forever." There was nothing to stop me. If I said it over and over again, I might come to believe it.

# THE PEAR TREE

*T*HEY WERE ONLY SUMMER PEOPLE, SO NO one paid them the least bit of attention. Ten years after Louis Stanley and his wife, Meg, had bought and restored the old Adams-Cooper farm, they were still thought of as strangers, asked for ID whenever they picked up packages at the post office, charged full price at the fish market even when buying cod or halibut at the end of the day. The blond woman who doted on her son, that's all the wife was, and the obnoxious husband was simply the fellow who fired Billy Griffon halfway through the renovation, before bringing in a team of carpenters from Rhode Island. No one invited the Stanleys to clam suppers or library fund-raisers. The family lived in Boston, after all, that was their home, and this town was only where they spent July and August, nothing more. Why would anyone bother to get to know them? Doing so would be like inviting the red-winged blackbirds in for supper, like fishing eels out of the bay in order to converse, like asking a red fox into the barn to spend the night. Different species, entirely. Best left to their own devices.

The son, Dean, could often be seen on a tire swing that had been rigged up with some rope that hung from the old pear tree in the front yard. You could see him from the road when you drove past: a shock of blond hair, long legs, a splash of movement on the other side of the lilac hedge. One year he seemed to have a dog, but the father probably couldn't abide the shedding and whining, and by the following summer, the dog was gone. Dean was an odd kid, and as he got older, he grew odder still. He spooked people. Some local boys would be fishing down at Halfway Pond, and they'd suddenly spy him, sitting all alone in the grass. He was spotted down at the bay at dusk as the fishermen came in to dock at the wharf—all by himself again, throwing stones, skimming them over the flat surface of the water as if the rest of the world didn't exist.

When the boy was fourteen, Billy Griffon was called in to turn the old summer kitchen into a garden shed, or at least that's what the husband had said. It wasn't often that a person had the chance to settle old scores, so Billy had agreed to come have a look. But when Billy arrived, Meg Stanley explained that she wanted the shed redone as a place for the boy. Billy Griffon took his time; he figured he'd charge the Stanleys double as reparation for the cost to his pride and his wallet all those years back when he was fired. It wasn't a small job, as a matter of fact. They wanted a built-in bunk bed, new windows and insulation, roofing, a desk with bookshelves. Meg Stanley came out and watched as Billy took the measurements. Billy was in no mood for nonsense; his wife, Lorri, had recently left him and moved down to Florida, and the price he was totaling up in his head for this renovation just kept getting higher. It was getting so that he might be able to go down to Florida for the month of January himself if he played this right.

"He doesn't like to be with us," Meg Stanley said of her boy.

She said it out of the blue, for no reason, and Billy Griffon wouldn't have been any more surprised if the mice in the field had suddenly addressed him.

"Boys that age," Billy Griffon blurted. Well, he had to say something, didn't he? The way she was standing there. The look on her face. He couldn't just ignore it. There was an echo in the shed, and his voice sounded strange. Sheep had been kept here in the past, and there was the bitter scent of animals and hay. "They're all idiots."

"I thought he'd be happier out here. You can smell the sea."

Meg had her arms crossed over her chest, and she looked so vulnerable standing there that Billy Griffon had the urge to put down his measuring tape and kiss her right on the mouth. Instead, he kept on with his figuring, and he drank the cool glass of lemonade Meg Stanley brought him, and the next day he sent her an estimate that was high, but not outrageous.

Straightaway, people in town told Billy he was a fool for taking the job. He knew they were right, but what did it matter? He'd been a fool before. Many times, indeed. He'd had no idea that Lorri was thinking of leaving him until she sprung her whole plan on him. All the same, it was a year when people were tightening their belts, when carpenters such as himself were begging for jobs, so that answered that. Meg Stanley approved his plans and the price, and when the husband, who seemed to know enough to keep his distance, sent a check for a third of the cost, Billy Griffon started bringing over lumber and supplies. Luckily, he wouldn't have much to do with the family, wouldn't even start the project until they'd moved back to the city. But on the day of his delivery he saw the boy out in the woods with a bow and arrow. Or at least that's what he thought he saw. He blinked and the boy was gone. Billy Griffon felt a chill go across him. The field to the left of the house was thick with blossoming sweet peas, and there was a droning sound in the air, bees and mosquitoes and those big horseflies that just won't leave a person alone. Behind the shed there were scrub pines, so it was impossible to spy the little pond at the rear of the property. If this had been Billy Griffon's place, he would have chopped down those pines, and the tangles of winterberry as well, and had a fine view from the house all the way to the pond. But this wasn't his house and it wasn't his business and he probably hadn't even seen the boy anyway.

Billy started working the second week in September. It was hot and beautiful and quiet, except for the call of the blackbirds. The pear tree out front was covered in new fruit, and the air smelled sweet. One afternoon, while Billy was reroofing the summer kitchen, the scent of tar overtook the sugary odor; all the same, he looked over at the yard. He saw that the pears had begun to turn color and that they were red. He kept thinking about those pears as he worked, and his mouth was watering. Usually, he was an honest man, but that afternoon he took two pears and let them ripen on the windowsill of his kitchen. Then Billy got it into his head that if he ate one something terrible would happen, and so he just watched the pears turn from red to scarlet to a blue-tinged crimson, then he threw them away.

At the Decoy Tavern people were saying Billy Griffon had been hypnotized, or maybe he had just found some of the killer marijuana that was said to grow wild in the fields on the Stanleys' property, planted years ago and all but for-gotten. Whatever the reason, he couldn't seem to stay away. True enough, he was taking his time with the bunk bed and the bookshelves, using good red oak; he was var-nishing the floor by hand and rebuilding the joists so stur-dily that a storm would have to be a hell-raiser if it aimed to knock down the shed. When he finished, there was trouble, just as everyone had predicted. Louis Stanley came down to inspect the completed project in December, and soon after, his lawyer fired off a note to Billy Griffon stat-ing that he had taken advantage of the Stanleys by using overpriced materials in a run-down shed. He'd overbuilt and overcharged. Therefore, Louis Stanley would only submit the second payment due, but not the third.

At the tavern no one looked up when Billy came in, which was exactly what had happened when Lorri left for Florida. Folks felt sorry for him in the way people always did for a well-meaning fool. Stop for a coyote on the side of the road, and expect to be bitten. Do it a second time, and expect to be pitied as well. Billy didn't mind, and he didn't bother to inform anyone that Stanley's wife had sent him the check for the remainder of what he was owed. That fact he kept to himself, even if he did look like a fool.

When people saw Billy's truck parked in the driveway of the Stanley house over the winter, they figured he was dis-mantling the shed, taking back all that good red oak to use somewhere else. They thought he was probably doing a little damage, and no one blamed him for seeking some retribution. But that wasn't it at all. He was watching the way the wind moved through the scrub pine. He was telling himself that feeling a chill doesn't make anything so, and stealing a red pear from an old tree couldn't cause misfortune any more than whistling through a blade of grass could call the eels out from the mud, creatures buried so deep you'd never know anything was there.

Billy Griffon stayed away after that. He'd gotten his money; he'd done his job. He forced himself not to park in the driveway. The next summer, he went up to Maine, to work on a huge job with some buddies. It was a mansion, really. His contribution was to fashion bird's-eye maple bookcases in the library, floor to ceiling. It was the kind of work he loved, but he took no pleasure from the job. When he got home to the Cape, he drove past the Stanleys' place, but the family had already moved back to Boston. Billy wondered if the boy had slept in the shed. If he'd smelled the sea at night; if he'd sat at the red-oak desk, if he'd been happier. He wondered if Meg Stanley had brought her boy cold lemonade, if she'd sat on the step and watched fireflies rise out of the field, if she'd thought about how much care had gone into everything he'd done.

The next summer, Dean Stanley was sixteen. He'd gotten his junior license, and he drove through town like a maniac, on a blue Honda motorcycle that echoed like a chain saw. Local women said they'd never let their sons drive around on such a deathtrap. All the same, they could tell, Dean wasn't one to listen or obey. He took risks, anyone could see that, racing into turns too quickly on the sandy back roads, careening through the rain without benefit of a slicker or a helmet. Everyone in town agreed, he'd wind up in trouble if he kept on this way. People wanted to dislike him, because of the father, but it was hard to dismiss Dean. He wasn't in the least like his father; he was completely himself. One day, walking home after work, Ivy Crosby from the post office saw the boy cradling a dead rabbit in the road. The poor creature had been run over by a Jackson's Fuel truck, a situation that probably happened fairly often. It was a trivial accident, but the boy was holding on to the rabbit and crying, real out-loud sobbing, in a way most people didn't wail even for their loved ones. It was hard for Ivy to get over seeing that poor boy like that, down on his knees, with that motorbike of his tossed onto the dirt shoulder of the road. Another time, Mickey Maguire over at the general store sold the boy a winning Lotto ticket. It was nothing much, three aces in a row, which added up to twenty dollars; nothing to get excited about. But the boy, Dean, had leapt over the counter and scared the hell out of Mickey with a huge bear hug.

"What the hell was he thinking?" Mickey Maguire said to folks down at the tavern. Why, Mickey's own children, Cody and Siggy, knew enough not to hug the old man, not when they were growing up and certainly not now. Mickey liked his personal space, especially in dealing with summer people. "What would he have done if he'd won fifty bucks?"

The next summer, the boy was seventeen; he'd crashed the motorbike in the city during the spring, and so he was walking again. He walked in the rain and late at night. You'd be on your way home from the drive-in or from supper with friends and there he'd be, moon-eyed, rambling, when everyone knew he had nowhere to go. No friends, no acquaintances, no suppers, no fund-raisers. Nothing. People were more afraid of running into him on the road than they were of hitting a deer head-on. Dean Stanley was a good-looking kid, lanky and lean, almost a man, but when you pulled up beside him as he went on his way, there was something off-putting in his expression. It was as though he was looking at something no one else saw. As though he was staring straight into the fire.

Louis Stanley didn't come down to their summer house much, perhaps a weekend or two, nothing more. The wife, Meg, still shopped at the fish store and went to the post office, but she seemed in a hurry, and appeared just as happy to have people treat her as though she were a stranger. When anyone said hello to her, she seemed to take a step back. Billy Griffon had seen her several times in town, and she didn't seem to recognize him. Billy had gotten a puppy, a black-Lab mix from the pound, and he tended to take the dog for walks in the woods near the Stanleys' place. One afternoon he all-out trespassed; he let the puppy splash around in the pond. But then he'd seen the woman, crying in the back yard, and he'd taken off running, the dog at his heels. Billy Griffon felt as if he'd stumbled into a bramble patch; as though there were nettles in his skin. He was feeling that something inevitable was about to happen. He was aware of how little he knew of this world, though he'd been in it for forty-five years. The dog was barking, and when Billy looked up he saw a big white bird in an old oak tree. He blinked, and then all he saw was a cloud.

It was a hot summer, hotter than usual, and things turned brown. Local people wished for fall, for leaves turning color and cool air sweeping in from Canada. When folks met at the ponds in the evenings they talked about the coming school year, and the way gardens were failing, and they also talked about the Stanley boy. The police had been called in to the house one night, and Cody Maguire, who worked with the sheriff and who'd never arrested anyone in his life, had found himself in the position of having to talk Dean out of the shed, where he'd barricaded himself. The kid had torn the bookshelves off the wall, and ripped out the built-in bunk as well, and piled it all against the door, vowing to defend himself with a butcher knife.

Meg Stanley had stood beside Cody as he pleaded with the boy to come out and have a talk. It had been a hot, starry night, filled with the sound of peepers and cicadas. Mrs. Stanley had been crying, and something about her fear was electric. Things could get out of hand. That much was clear. The heat was sickening, too sweet somehow. Cody Maguire said he'd have to phone in to the sheriff to get a team in from the next town over, and that's when Meg Stanley, who had called in the emergency in the first place, told him to get off her property. She had an expression on her face like she knew where this was going, and she just wasn't going to let it get there. She could handle the boy, she insisted. If Cody had been more experienced he would never have left Mrs. Stanley there alone. But he was only half a dozen years older than Dean, and he was grateful to be released. He hightailed it to the patrol car, and drove back to the station; even when it was over, he had to compose himself for nearly half an hour out in the parking lot before his nerves were steady enough for him to make his report.

After that incident, Billy Griffon made sure to drive by on his way home from work. If he saw the light on in the kitchen, he figured everything was all right. One evening, he phoned over at the Stanleys', and when Meg answered, it took him a moment to gather his thoughts. He said he was just wondering if his work was holding up. If any more renovations were needed he could come by and see to them; it would be no trouble at all.

Meg Stanley took a breath before she answered, and for an instant Billy thought she would say, *Yes, I need help, come over right now*. But she only thanked him for his kindness and told him they didn't need any work done. "I loved the bookshelves," she said before she hung up. "I should have told you that before."

Billy Griffon was the one who found the boy, and some people said that was just his luck. He was driving home from the beach after letting his dog go for a run, going past the Stanleys' like he always did. It was evening, and shadowy, and the light was funny, with streaks of gold and inky blue. The wind had picked up, and some branches skittered across the road, and all at once Billy's dog, riding in the back of the truck, started barking. The shadow was across their lawn, where the pear tree stood. Billy Griffon blinked and saw nothing. He blinked again, and saw red. He thought about those pears he had stolen, and about people who couldn't sleep at night. He thought he would run as fast as he could, and it still wouldn't be fast enough. How, he wondered, would he explain what had happened to Meg Stanley? The words would tumble out of his mouth one after another, like stones. The words would sink down so far they would never come back, down into the well, drowning them both before he was done.

The dog ran across the lawn, into the pool of shadow. The air smelled like something burning, and like low tide. Billy's dog barked and tried to jump up, and Billy had to grab him by the collar. He'd named the dog Hugo, but now he just called him Pup. *Down,* Billy Griffon said. *Down, Pup.*

He didn't know what he was supposed to do, but he

knew he couldn't have her see this. The boy had hanged himself from one of the top branches, his belt tied around a strong, thick limb that was sure to hold. Feathers were on the ground below him, as if the birds nesting in the tree had all taken flight at once. There was a single line of gold in the sky now. The rest had all faded.

Billy took hold of his dog's collar and brought him back to the truck; he put Hugo into the front seat, then went round to the back for his toolbox. He grabbed his ladder and a saw. He felt dizzy in the golden light, with the dry, brown heat of August around him. He thought about the summer when the boy was fourteen, when Meg had held her arms around herself, when he'd wanted to kiss her on the mouth. He didn't give a damn if it was a criminal offense to tamper with what had gone on here. He propped up the ladder and cut the boy down. It was quick and horrible work, but the thud in the grass was softer than he had imagined. Like a feather falling.

Billy Griffon could hear his dog barking, locked up in the truck, as he walked on to the house. Every step he'd taken in his life was nothing compared to this. Years from now, he'd remember the sweet peas that grew by the door, he'd remember that a catbird had called from its perch in a scrub pine. The carpenters from Rhode Island had done a lousy job, he saw that now, and the French doors they'd put in were crooked. Billy would have been more careful. He would have taken his time. When she told him to get rid of the pear tree, he wouldn't try to argue with her the way another man might have. He'd just come out here to the property after the leaves had all dropped off, after the fruit had littered the ground, and he'd chop the damned thing down.

# THE SUMMER
# KITCHEN

PEOPLE BUY HOUSES FOR ALL SORTS OF
reasons, for shelter, for solace, for love, for
investment. Katherine and Sam bought
their summer house because they were
drowning, and this was the first solid ground
they thought they might be able to hold on
to. It was a farm on the outermost reaches of
the Cape with white clapboards and green
shutters. Two hundred years earlier, oysters
had been stored in wooden tubs in the fields
beyond the house; turnips and asparagus
and sweet peas had grown here. The realtor
told them that elsewhere in town the soil
was so sandy little could grow, but this land

was rich; years of farm manure, and a layer of fertilizer formed from smashed oyster shells, had brought forth acres of peach and apple trees that bloomed pink in the spring and lilacs so tall a person could completely disappear beneath their branches and hear nothing but the humming of bees.

That's what they wanted, Katherine and Sam both, to crawl beneath green leaves and branches and hide from the year they'd had, the year they were still stuck inside on the day they decided to spend their savings on the farm. They were rapt as the realtor told them there was a hillside of blueberries, the low-growing kind so perfect for jam. There was a fenced garden filled with June strawberries and summer raspberries so tart a single taste could make one's mouth pucker, along with plenty of room for a vegetable patch of their own making, not that their children— a boy and a girl, Walker and Emma, aged ten and six—could be talked into eating lettuce and cucumbers, even the homegrown variety.

Of course, they had to imagine all this, as it was January when they stood there. Still, they made an offer on the spot, on impulse, foolishly paying the asking price for a house no one else wanted, one that had been on the market for over a year. But Katherine and Sam were desperate, two drowning people out in the cold with the realtor, watching the sun go down on what would soon be their land. A summer house was never a necessary purchase, but this was a particularly rash decision, a foolhardy whim in a time of chaos, made at the exact hour when most people knew to avoid any serious change. Still, they went ahead with it, a leap of faith designed to convince themselves that, even though there was ice on the ground and a land-scape of bleak, bare trees, there would indeed be summers to come, a time when blueberry jam would be simmering on the stovetop, when everyday life was restored.

They'd been released from their duty at the hospital for a single day, this icy afternoon on the Cape that smelled like salt and straw, rescued by dear friends from out of town who took one look at them and insisted they go away and enjoy themselves. These friends had no idea that Katherine and Sam no longer enjoyed themselves, and had in fact stopped talking to each other months earlier. On the ride down to the Cape, for instance, they hadn't both-ered to speak, even though this was their day off. There seemed no point in conversation that didn't pertain to their daughter's medical condition. As they drove they looked out the window in silence, two stick figures who continued to exist even though every bit of life had been drained out of them, bled dry by panic and fear.

And yet, when they'd walked down the dirt driveway to the farm, they'd both become giddy. In a fit of crazed good humor, a mood so unusual it felt as though they'd been drugged, they had made their offer, and in doing so they had opened themselves up to hope, to believing that Emma would turn seven in June, that she would pick blueberries later in the summer, make jam, run past the stretch of peach trees alongside her brother, Walker; that she would survive.

They nearly forgot about the house in the spring, when Emma was so improved. It was a delight to have her back from the hospital, to regain a bit of their normal existence, to speak to each other, now and again, about ordinary things. Emma had lost all her hair the previous fall, when her chemotherapy had begun. Katherine had bought her daughter a dozen pretty hats, then locked herself in the bathroom to cry for the loss of Emma's long, blond hair. Now the child's hair had begun to grow back, first in a fuzz, then, astoundingly, in black tufts. Emma's prognosis was excellent, and yet Katherine couldn't allay her panic. Emma's newly grown black hair made it seem as though she had fallen under a spell. Such things happened, the oncologist assured Katherine. Straight hair turned curly, fine hair grew in coarse and thick. All the same, it seemed like an enchantment to Katherine. The alchemy of how one thing became another was a puzzle that could never be solved: light became dark, joy turned to sorrow, and then— for the lucky, for the few—to joy once more.

As for Emma, she didn't mind the new color of her hair. If anything, she seemed to like the fact that it was now black, with waves that hadn't been there before. Perhaps she valued the change as a sign that she had walked through fire and was still here, an announcement that this was a brand-new Emma, a girl who was well, one so strong she could arm-wrestle with her brother, and nearly beat him at the game.

"I could be a witch for Halloween," Emma said thoughtfully as she appraised herself in the bathroom mirror. "I could be a Gypsy queen."

Katherine, of course, never mentioned to anyone, not even to Sam, that when she caught sight of Emma in a darkened hallway the child no longer appeared to be her daughter, that good-natured blonde girl nothing could harm. She was someone different now, the little girl who knew more than she should, a shadow, a sprite, a witch, a queen.

THEY MOVED INTO THE HOUSE ON THE FOURTH OF July weekend. Having plowed through traffic jams, they were sticky with sweat as they unloaded the rental truck. They'd packed up some old furniture from their first apartment and a few pieces Sam had inherited from his mother: a dining-room table, a sideboard, a dilapidated chair so comfortable the children argued over who would sit in it first.

"I think we're insane," Sam said when he stopped to survey the house. He was a big no-nonsense man who rarely did anything on impulse.

"We can sell it next year. Don't worry," Katherine told him, although what she really meant was: *Don't walk out on me now*. All through the year she'd been afraid he might do that, be so overwhelmed by the possibility of tragedy that he'd leave before it actually happened. "Just this summer," she begged. "Then we'll see."

THAT WEEKEND THEY DISCOVERED THERE WERE quirks about the property. They learned soon enough, because Walker, out to explore the tall grass in their field, came back shouting that there was a tick in his hair. There were burrs stuck to his trousers, too, and he had narrowly avoided a rather large patch of poison ivy. Surprises existed inside as well, none of them pleasant. Pipes rattled, water tasted rusty, two burners on the stove didn't work at all. The house hadn't been lived in for more than a year, so it wasn't a shock to find mice in the hall. But they were only babies, cute little things, and Emma threw a fit when Sam said he would set out poison.

"Don't you care about the value of life?" Emma had said to her father.

People said long stays in the hospital could do this to a child, make her grow up fast, allow her to see what others might not. Certainly, this was true with the Gypsy queen, who collected each tiny mouse in an egg cup, and carried them to the tick-infested field, where they'd certainly be scooped up by hawks in no time flat. This little witch considered matters of life and death as she danced around the blueberry bushes, willing them to bear fruit, as she rescued spiders, watered the old strawberry plants, which were withered and spent. Katherine's own black-haired wonder girl, back from the brink, watching for fireflies every night, as if they were the most marvelous sight in the universe, as if just being alive was more than enough.

KATHERINE HADN'T BEEN THINKING MUCH ABOUT Walker. Nobody had, as a matter of fact, until he started to talk about the blackbird. Katherine had quit her job at the library when Emma was first diagnosed. Sam was a lawyer, and had to go back to town after the holiday. Right away, Katherine fell into a schedule of spending all her time with Emma. They pretended their life on the farm was an opera. Though Katherine was known for her off-key voice, and Emma wasn't much better, they sang every request: *Pass the peas! Look at the mockingbird! Do you want bubbles in your bath!*

"You guys are crazy," Walker had muttered. And then, pointedly, to Katherine, "Everyone knows you can't sing a note."

Walker had laid claim to a shed in the field, which he'd

turned into a fort. He had very little patience with his mother and sister, and very little time to waste on them. Soon enough, he'd learned to pull ticks off without any help and burn them till they popped. He became adept at avoiding burrs and poison ivy. He was sunburned and rangy and hungry all the time. It was as if his body was preparing for a growth spurt to come; as if Walker, too, was preparing to become someone new.

It wasn't until the middle of July that Katherine noticed that her son had become secretive. He had lost some tender quality of childishness, overnight, it seemed. When Emma, always a rescuer, found a toad in their garden and made a house in a hole near the porch, Walker asked her why she was bothering with what was nothing more than a good meal for the owl that lived in their woods.

"Toad à la mode," he had said, and Emma, so busy saving any creature she came across, had cried at the notion that her toad was nothing more than a mouthful, a meal.

"Do you have to behave so miserably?" Katherine had said.

"What do you care?" Walker had stalked away, back to the field where the grass grew so tall it was indeed possible to disappear from sight.

Talk of the blackbird began that same week. When a peach pie was found smashed to bits on the kitchen floor, with crust scattered everywhere, Walker insisted a huge bird had flown in through the window. When the laundry out on the line was found strewn about on the ground, Walker declared this same bird had picked the clothespins from the line one by one.

"Well, tell that bird I'm going to pluck his feathers if I catch him. Tell him to stop being so troublesome."

That day, Walker disappeared for the entire afternoon. When Katherine couldn't find him on her own, and the sun was beginning to go down, she frantically phoned the local police department. An officer came to the house to take down a description of Walker: ten and a half, fair hair, sunburned, skinny, angrier than most boys his age, probably wearing a bathing suit and sneakers.

As it turned out, Walker came back soon after the police car left. By then Katherine was so frantic she'd phoned Sam twice and had bitten her nails to the quick. Twice, she'd searched the woods, and had mistakenly walked through a patch of nettles. She'd been in a panic, and now here was Walker, sauntering up the drive in the fading light.

"Where were you?" Katherine cried. She grabbed him by the shoulders, too fierce, too harsh.

"I walked to the beach. I left you a note on the door." Walker pulled away. Lately, he couldn't stand to be touched. They went to the door and there was indeed a silver thumbtack on the ground. But no note. "The blackbird must have taken it. He's a practical joker."

"Right." Katherine's tone was clipped. She'd been imagining horrible things as she'd searched through the woods. She knew she should be relieved, but instead she was angry now, too.

"It was him," Walker insisted.

Later in the week, when Katherine and Emma were clearing out brambles from around the blueberry bushes, Katherine asked if Emma had ever seen the bird Walker blamed for everything that went wrong.

"I know the blackbird thinks it's funny to steal things."

"How do you know?"

Emma looked at Katherine with a serious expression. "Walker said so."

They'd met their closest neighbor recently, Josephine Brooks, who had lived her whole life in the house next door. They'd already promised Miss Brooks their extra fruit. It seemed there'd be plenty: the berries had already turned from green to a dull gray-blue. It was time to throw nets over the bushes, to protect them from birds.

"And he's different from other blackbirds," Emma added as she worked. "He's white."

"I see."

Miss Brooks had told them that Walker's fort was used as a summer kitchen in times past. Most of their neighbors remembered the smell of sugar rising in the air whenever jam was simmered. There were wonderful preserves back then, made from beach plums and apricots and peaches and these same blueberries that had always grown wild.

Sure enough, when Katherine checked, she found there was a fireplace in the shed, with two metal posts that could hold a large pot. She noticed that Walker had taken the broom from the house and had swept the summer kitchen clean. But there was something else that she saw: a secret kept, an old bow and a set of arrows, the sort of thing Katherine had always forbidden as too dangerous. She felt as though she was well within her rights when she took the bow and arrows and set them in the trash.

But in the morning, when she got ready to go to the dump, the bow and arrows were gone. Not only that, the vegetable garden she and Emma had worked so hard to fill with tomatoes and cucumbers and peas had been dug up haphazardly, so that the vines were draped in the dirt and the new tomatoes had been shaken off, then smashed into worthless pulp.

Katherine went up to Walker's bedroom, angrier than she wanted to be. He looked younger when he was asleep, dirt-streaked, his scalp showing through his clipped hair. Last year, when she told him Emma had been diagnosed with leukemia, he'd been straight-faced; nothing showed through.

*No she hasn't*, he'd said to Katherine. *You're a liar*.

Now she woke him and asked what had happened to the garden. Walker shrugged, hazy with sleep.

"It must have been the blackbird."

"I see. You had nothing to do with it. And did this bird give you the bow and arrows, too?"

"I found them. Under the floor of the fort."

This might in fact be true. Miss Brooks had told Katherine that there had been a teen-aged boy who'd last lived here, and he might easily have fooled around with bows and arrows.

"Well, you should have told me. Now I feel that I can't trust you."

"That's fine." Walker got out of bed. He let the quilt drop on the floor. He looked taller than he had the day before. "That makes us equal."

Later, Katherine followed at a distance when Walker and Emma went into the woods. He had set up a target far past the field, where the coyotes whose young they heard yapping at night must live. The target was a bale of hay, most likely taken from the neighbor down the road, who had a corral and two ponies.

"Let's pretend I'm the Gypsy queen." Emma quickly made herself comfortable on a fallen log covered with moss. In woods so dark, her hair didn't look quite so black. "You have to do everything I say and win a prize that you present to me."

"I'll be a knight," Walker agreed. "No one's ever beaten me at my own game. Not in all the land."

He sounded so young that Katherine felt like crying. She felt as though she were the evil queen, the one who sent the hero to a terrible fate, who asked him to collect golden apples, though he might meet an untimely death when attempting such an impossible task, when he might be lost forevermore.

"What were you and Walker doing in the woods today?" Katherine asked later, after Emma had taken her bath and they were saying good night.

"Nothing." And when she realized that wasn't enough, Emma added, "Playing queens and knights."

No mention of the bow and arrows or the target made out of hay.

"And did you see the blackbird?"

Emma shook her head. "But Walker said it would try to steal my hair clips, so I put them in my pocket. He's white, you know, like snow."

"Emma, you know there's no such thing."

These days, there was still sunlight at bedtime, and now flashes of drowsy light slipped around the window shade. Josephine Brooks' lawn had been mowed earlier in the day, and there was the scent of cut grass. Katherine had taken to talking to Sam late at night; she'd bring the phone into bed with her, where she could whisper about her concerns.

"They both insist it's real," Katherine told Sam. "At least they agree."

THE NEXT DAY WAS JAM DAY. THE BLUEBERRIES HAD all been picked, the twigs and leaves cleaned away. Katherine and Emma went into town for jam jars, and afterward

Katherine made a stop at Town Hall. Miss Brooks had been pruning the old lilacs in the morning, and before they left for town, Katherine told her about the renegade bird that was supposedly doing so much damage; Josephine didn't seem surprised. In fact, she was the one who suggested the stop at Town Hall.

"Your boy's not the first to have seen the bird. Supposedly, it was the pet of the sailor boy who lived in your house. The poor boy went off to sea with his father and he never came back. But the blackbird did. Or at least, that's what people say."

"Well, it's nonsense." Katherine laughed.

"A storm came up, if I remember correctly."

She had, Katherine soon discovered. The sailor who had built their house and his ten-year-old son had disappeared into the center of a huge, unexpected nor'easter. The boy's name had been Isaac, and right away Katherine wished she didn't know that fact. It made him seem realer, a boy who had run down the twisted steps from the second floor every morning, who swept out the summer kitchen on hot days, who could catch a bluefish in seconds flat.

"It's dusty here," Emma said. She looked at the book of records Katherine had pulled down from the shelf. "Who are you reading about?"

"A little sailor boy who disappeared in a storm. Isaac Hadley. He was only ten."

"That was young to die."

"It was."

Sunlight was pouring in through the dusty window, and more dust rose when Katherine closed the book.

"You're the ones who live in the sailor's house," the clerk said when Katherine returned the record book. "You know what they say, put out salt if you want to chase that old blackbird away. Or is it that salt will bring a sailor home from the sea?"

"We don't want to get rid of him," Emma said. They went out to the car, which was hot as blazes. "I'll bet Isaac was scared in that storm," Emma said thoughtfully. "Everything he saw was dark. Black ocean. Black sky. Only the blackbird was white. Blackbirds aren't supposed to be that color, but this one was. You know what would have made it better for Isaac?" Emma added. "If someone had been there with him, the way you were always there with me in the hospital."

"You know this is all just pretend, right?" Emma looked so healthy now; there were streaks of sun in her dark hair. She was long past her seventh birthday, a touchstone date, a step into the future. "There are no such things as ghosts, if that's what you're thinking. Not of boys and not of birds. There's only the here and now, Emma."

"And the once was and the soon is going to be," Emma insisted.

Katherine laughed and joined in. "And the should be and the could be and the would be."

They sang all the way home. Then they boiled the jam jars and carried the ingredients to the summer kitchen. As it turned out, it was the hottest day of the year, ninety-six in the shade, and much hotter once they got the fire going in the shed's fireplace. They used old peach wood and oak branches and kindling Emma collected in a wicker basket. Walker saw the smoke billowing from the chimney, and came running. When he realized they were using his fort as a kitchen, he was furious.

"You want everything that belongs to me. This place was mine," he said, before he turned and stomped back into the woods.

When the jam was done, they had twenty-four jars, one for every hour of the day, Katherine said. They piled up their finished product in the shade, then carried the cooking pot and what was left of the sugar through the woods. They were hot and sweaty and their mouths were blue from the extra fruit they had eaten. They looked for Walker, but there was nothing as far as the eye could see, except for swarms of mosquitoes. There was the evening star above them. Katherine asked Emma what she was wishing for.

"What I'd like most of all," Emma said. "Is for you to love Walker."

"But I do!" Katherine was shocked. "Of course I love him."

"I mean so it shows." They had passed onto the lawn,

each one holding a handle of the cooking pot. In the sunlight, Emma's hair glinted golden. "Do it so he knows."

LATER, KATHERINE WENT BACK THROUGH THE WOODS and loaded all of the jars of jam into a cardboard box. She could see why Walker liked the summer kitchen. The heat was fading, so that the day already felt like a memory. There were fireflies drifting through the falling dark, and a few luminous clouds in the sky up above. Walker hadn't come down for dinner; he'd stayed up in his room, exhausted, bad-tempered. Now, as Katherine walked home through the dusky woods, lugging the heavy jars, she thought, *He's ten. The same age as the boy lost at sea.*

Katherine went directly upstairs, where the rooms were hot and close. She had the feeling that love was an anchor, that it could save you when you were drowning, that all you had to do was hold tight.

Walker was sprawled out on his bed, gazing out his window as fireflies floated by. One blink and they were gone. One radiant beam of light, and then nothing but the dark. Katherine lay down beside her son. He smelled of dirt and summer; he smelled exactly like the woods beyond their house, sharp and sweet and green.

"What do you want?" He didn't even look at her. Not a glance.

"I thought I'd sing you to sleep," Katherine said.

Walker laughed, but the sound was dry, like something breaking. "You can't sing. Everybody knows that."

"You're right." Katherine thought of the little sailor on his sinking ship, out in the coldest ocean. She hoped there were stars out that night, something to guide him. "I know I can't," she admitted. "But I thought I'd try."

# WISH YOU WERE
# HERE

*I*T WAS A TERRIBLE BIRTHDAY PRESENT,
the absolute last thing Emma would have
wanted. To turn thirty was awful enough. To
turn thirty after a divorce, with no child, and
no career to speak of, other than the teaching job she'd fallen into at the very same
school she'd attended as a teenager, now,
that was downright dreadful. But of course
she couldn't say any of this out loud—she
had to be grateful just to be alive. She'd
nearly died when she was six, or so her
brother, Walker, told her often enough. He
showered her with more details than she'd
ever wanted to know: how lucky she was,

how other children with the exact same diagnosis had died in less than six months. Walker was a pediatrician now, with three children of his own and a great store of knowledge about leukemia. It was his specialty, actually, and he was thrilled and proud at the strides medicine had made. As for Emma's illness, the treatments she'd had had cured her, but it also seemed likely they might have left her unable to have a child.

"That wouldn't happen these days," Walker had told her. "They gave patients megadoses of chemo back when you were in treatment."

Well, maybe that was fate. Maybe she was meant to be alone. She was a runner, and wasn't that the habit of a person who preferred to be on her own? She was no team player; she didn't even care for tennis. She liked to run along the river when the sky was still dark. She thought of herself as a star shooting along Storrow Drive, measuring her strides against the flow of the Charles, racing toward Commonwealth Avenue. At that early hour, Boston seemed like Alexandria or Paris, mysterious and inky, a city filled with smoke and possibility. In the spring, there were scores of magnolias, like wild birds captured and caged. The scent of lilacs was dizzying.

The route that Emma took had once been underwater, filled in a hundred years earlier with silt and mud, but watery still. Puddles collected. The air had a green tint. Ducks nested in the reeds. Emma was a city girl; to her, ducks were wildlife. Reeds were definitely flora enough. She liked soot, and heat, and grime, and, she was beginning to realize, if she didn't actually like her aloneness, she was at least comforted by it. She should be grateful; she knew, she knew. She should be thrilled just to be alive. So why was it she preferred to expect nothing? Why was it she felt she'd already ruined everything? As though her life had somehow ended? There were times when she felt so insubstantial it was almost as though people could walk right through her. Lately, she couldn't visit Walker and his family without becoming sick to her stomach.

"You're allergic to us, Sis," Walker decreed, but that wasn't it at all. If anything, Emma was allergic to herself. Sometimes, she broke out in a rash, and she knew the reason why. It was punishment for what she should have felt and didn't. Deep down, she wasn't grateful. That was the thing. Deep down, she wished she was six and it was the day before her diagnosis, the hour when she still believed in things.

She was therefore expecting a horrible birthday, but she wasn't expecting the package her mother sent up from Florida, where Emma's parents had moved the year before. It was a manila envelope that arrived, too large to be a birthday card, too small to be a sweater or a shawl. When she'd turned twenty-eight, the year of her divorce, Emma had slept around. It was a shameful year; one of her worst. Her husband, Dave, had told her he felt as though he'd married a ghost. She was so unengaged, he blamed her for the way he'd turned to other women. After they broke up, Emma had wanted to prove that she was indeed alive. She had brought home men she didn't care about, as if for spite. She had done things she'd be too embarrassed ever to admit aloud, even to her best friend, Callie. The worst instance? She'd had sex with someone else's husband in the couple's marriage bed. She'd seen a photograph of the other woman, the wife, and her children in the bedroom. The woman had been laughing; she'd thought she was happy, and afterward Emma had felt like writing her a note: *Run away*, that's what she wanted to tell this man's wife. *What could he possibly be worth if he slept with me?*

Perhaps to heap more punishment upon herself, she went on to her next humiliation and took up with Alex Mott, who taught history, and who, in many ways, she despised for his rigidity and his contempt for his students. All the same, she'd gone into the utility closet with him during school hours, and she'd dropped to her knees just to hear what he would sound like when he climaxed. It wasn't much, that's what she'd discovered. It sounded as though someone was strangling, although whether that someone was herself or Alex, she wasn't sure.

During the year she'd been twenty-nine, Emma had had two dates and no sex. Frankly, she hadn't even been approached for sex, except for that horrible Alex, who looked at her in a way that made her feel like running. Emma now had tremendous sympathy for the girls in her school who'd made the mistake of going too far with the wrong boy, girls who'd had their phone numbers written on bathroom walls. She thought people looked at her oddly during faculty meetings. Perhaps they all knew she'd had degrading, unsatisfying sex with someone she despised in the utility closet, or perhaps they simply disapproved of the fact that she graded some of the girls in her class far too easily, giving A's to those who didn't deserve them, merely because they'd been treated unfairly in matters of the heart.

Emma took to running at the lunch hour just so she wouldn't have to talk to Alex Mott or anyone else in the faculty cafeteria. She felt like a shadow-woman, a vapor in the hallways at school, a fleeting bit of light racing along the river. Thirty, she supposed, would mean the end of all human contact. Especially once school let out. Usually, she traveled in the summers, often to France, where she rented cheap apartments in August and went running for hours every day. But this summer, she'd made no plans. It seemed she hadn't the fortitude to call a travel agent or phone a rental agent. She had stopped answering her phone when it rang. Who would be calling her? What did she have to say to anyone? So here she was in the heat of summer, alone on her birthday, which had fallen on a beautiful blue day. She was sitting on the floor of her apartment, a woman of thirty who should have been glad just to be alive, with a manila envelope in her hands. A gift from her parents.

There were papers inside the envelope, a mishmash of documents, signed by both her mother and father. Emma wasn't quite certain what it all was until she read the note her mother had enclosed: *Happy birthday, baby girl. This was always meant for you.*

It was the farm they'd bought down at the edge of the Cape when Emma's treatment was through. The very edge of the world, Emma's father used to say when they drove out from Boston for the summer, and, certainly, it had seemed that way. It was the light that Emma remembered as so very different from city light, thin and yellow, with flecks of gold as the afternoon stretched on. Apricot light, her mother used to call it. Peach light. Summertime light that made a person forget gray skies and city life. The air was sweeter there, the cardinals were a deeper scarlet than their city cousins, and when the crickets called, it was possible to feel the vibration of their song. Each time they opened the car doors and crossed the grass, it was as though they had stepped off the globe, as though the world had stopped turning, as though they might, for a little while at least, be safe.

Emma and her mother had made jam every summer, up until Emma was fifteen and Walker was eighteen and the two put forth a unified front, arguing to stay in town and get summer jobs. Really, they were selfish teenagers who wanted to hang out with their friends. They were in the bright apex of their lives, when the past was quite meaningless and the present all that mattered. Until then, making jam had been a tradition, the one thing Emma and her mother would do together, even when they weren't getting along. Every year it was a new variety: blueberry, strawberry, blackberry, mint, corn relish, and, on autumn weekends, Concord grape made from the wild vines beyond the pond. But that was ages ago. For some time, Emma and Walker had been suggesting their parents sell the place. Walker went down with his family only for a week or two in August, Emma hadn't been there for years, and the renters they'd recently had had been nothing but trouble. There'd been a fire one summer, when some idiots used the outhouse as a place to set up their barbecue. The poor old outhouse, unused, but still appreciated for the valiant way it held up the woody trumpet vine, had been turned to cinders. The applewood floors in the kitchen had been refinished so many times they were nearly worn away. One summer some children, whose family had rented the place for an entire month, had felt proprietary enough to carve their initials into the window ledges on the second floor, where Walker and Emma had had their bedrooms tucked under the eaves.

"I told you you were the favorite," Walker said when Emma called to tell him of her unwanted windfall.

"I was the one to be pitied," Emma said.

"Never," Walker told her. "Not you, kiddo."

"You have to say that. You're a physician and can't do any harm."

"I'm your brother. I could tease you unmercifully if I wanted to, harmful or not. Enjoy the house."

Emma planned to check out the farm, set it in order, and sell it as quickly as possible. She was practical that way, and if her parents said now that the house belonged to her, she could sell it if she so desired. To this end, Emma's best friend and old college roommate, Callie Hecht, was enlisted to take a trip with her, back to the edge of the world.

"Perfect," Callie had said right away when Emma phoned. "It will be Midsummer's Eve. We can call up some spirits."

Perfect also for Callie to leave behind her son and her daughter and her husband, David. The good David, they called him, as opposed to Emma's ex, the evil David, the David with no heart, the one who was convinced he was living with a ghost. Callie was also leaving behind her family's unruly black Lab, three cats, and a house in Nyack. She was more than grateful for the downtime, and swore she didn't mind going out of her way, driving to Boston to pick up Emma. All the more time to be alone, she enthused.

"You want alone?" Emma laughed. "Welcome to my life."

Callie double-parked on Commonwealth, and they packed up her station wagon with sleeping bags and pillows, along with huge amounts of groceries and bottles of wine, flashlights, candles, powdered milk, ground French-roast coffee.

"We're only going for a weekend," Callie reminded her friend.

"Trust me," Emma had said. "You'll see. There's nothing there."

THE FIRST THING EMMA NOTICED WHEN THEY PULLED into the long dirt driveway was how abandoned the place looked. She was surprised to realize that the image of the house she kept in mind, even now, was the house as it had been that first year. She was glad that her mother couldn't see what had happened to it. So much paint had flaked off the shingles, the house barely looked white. Part of the roof had flown off in a spring nor'easter, and the old summer kitchen had collapsed in the same storm and was now little more than a bundle of sticks. The unwieldy sweet peas had so invaded the field that anyone wishing to get to the other side would need to wield an ax in order to walk through.

"I see what you mean," Callie said. "This is bleak." Then she and Emma got out of the car, and Callie shouted "Strawberries!" and took off running in the direction of the field.

"Watch out for poison ivy!" Emma yelled after her, but

it was too late. Callie was already deep into the poison ivy that always bordered the strawberry patch. She was beginning to itch when it came time to unload the car.

"Well, at least I got us dessert," Callie said. "In exchange for my pains."

The house was cold, the way abandoned houses are, the air inside cooler than the temperature outside. Breathe out, and the air turned to crystals. Breathe in, and it chilled to the bone. They opened the windows, let in some heat and some sun, then made up the beds in the attic. There was evidence of mice, and the rooms needed to be swept. And all the while they were working, Callie was itching like mad. In the afternoon, Emma drove down to the general store, in search of calamine lotion. Siggy Maguire was working the register, as she had for years. When Siggy realized who Emma was she inquired after her mother, then told Emma that last summer the renters they'd had had complained to everyone on the road that the house was haunted. They said a white bird had frightened their son; when the teen-aged girls in the family started fooling around with a Ouija board they'd scared themselves silly, and the whole family had packed up and left.

"Good riddance," Emma said smartly.

"My sentiments exactly." Siggy was very no-nonsense, and she'd always been so. "Tell your mom I'm still picking blueberries up on your hill like she said I could. They're not going to waste. If I had the time, I'd clear out some of that poison ivy near the strawberry patch. I saw you lost a lot of trees and that shed of yours finally went down. Your mom always called one of the Crosby boys to take care of such things. I'll do it for you if you like."

Emma agreed, thanked Siggy, then bought more than she should have to be polite. Along with the calamine lotion, she added another bottle of wine and some plum cakes, baked by Siggy's sister-in-law, Elizabeth, just to be neighborly.

"I remember how cute you were when you first walked in here," Siggy said as Emma was leaving. "Your hair was just starting to grow back."

"I must have looked terrible." Emma laughed, embarrassed. "Cueball."

"Oh, no. You were cute as could be. That's why I could still pick you out. That sort of thing makes an impression."

What sort of thing was that? Emma wondered as she drove back to the house. She took the long route, along the bay. Everything smelled like salt and heat. The eelgrass shimmered and the sand was covered with little scrambling crabs. Today was the longest day of the year, and, oddly, Emma was glad for that. She wanted the day to last. She pulled over onto the side of the road and closed her eyes and tried to imagine walking into the general store at the age of seven, with her scraggly hair, unself-conscious. Was she glad to be alive at that moment? Did she thank Siggy Maguire for the Milky Way candy bar she was given for free, just for being her cute self on that summer day? Just for having survived?

Emma got out of her car. She could hear the drone of the cicadas. She planned to go for a short run, but instead wound up racing along the inlets of the bay for over an hour. There was sand in her shoes when she got back to the house. Her skin was shiny with sweat and salt.

"Thank God you're back," Callie said by way of a greeting. Itch-ridden Callie had actually been waiting for Emma at the front door. Her arms were covered with poison-ivy bumps, even though she'd washed with the bar of brown soap she'd found in the bathroom. Emma poured calamine lotion onto cotton and watched as Callie covered the rashy spots. "This place is hellish," Callie said. "While I was lying down I heard something underneath me. I shouldn't have looked, but I did. There was a mouse under the bed. I screamed and it ran away. And then I ran away as well, and here I am, waiting for you."

Emma laughed as she put away the provisions she'd bought at the store.

"It's not funny. You were right about this place. It really is a wreck. There's no hot water, did you know that? And the groceries you brought? Well, good luck, because the refrigerator isn't working."

Emma went to the fridge, moved it out from the wall, fiddled with the plug, then adjusted the temperature.

"*Voilà*," she said. "Modern life."

Callie was not impressed. "I'm lying down. If that mouse comes back, I'll kill it. I swear I will. It is true what they say, this day really is endless."

This longest day of the year was known as Johnmas, or Sailor's Eve, a good time to ask for whatever it was a person wanted most. It was the day that often marked the time sailors were in the middle of a sea voyage; most likely what they wanted most was to come home again. They wanted the sight of oak trees and of willows, the taste of sweet green water that would quench their thirst, the sound of a woman's voice, no matter what her tone might be. When Callie went to lie down, Emma went out to explore the grounds and see what other damage she could find. Tomorrow she would ask Siggy for the name of a trustworthy real-estate agent, but for now she simply enjoyed the quiet. The pond was brackish, but there were still those Egyptian water lilies Emma had always liked. They looked like bits of sunlight on the dark-green water. Bits and pieces of gold.

She walked over to explore the field of sweet peas. It would take a tractor to get rid of them all. Emma startled the finches feeding on purple thistle as she walked along the edges of the field; she could hear a skittering in the tall grass—field mice, most probably, or those little voles that made their way underground to the tenderest garden shoots. Halfway through the field, Emma tripped over a clod or a bump. She bent and found something odd: a row of undersized turnips were growing there. Emma got down on her hands and knees and dug them out. She took the turnips back to the house, got out an old cookbook, and had a steamy broth cooking by the time Callie came down from her nap.

"Yum," Callie said, but when she took her first spoonful of the soup, she burst into tears. "I miss my family," she admitted. "Can you believe it? I must be crazy."

Emma tasted the turnip broth—just a spoonful, really— but her eyes grew moist as well. Crying turnips, truthteller's turnips, sweet, but somewhat difficult to eat. Emma had the feeling that if she took another spoonful she'd soon be under some sort of spell.

"Maybe we're meant to have a pizza." Emma spilled the broth down the sink, and the two friends went out to a local bar, where they ordered a clam pizza and a large pitcher of beer, and soon felt much better. On the ride back to the farm, the sky was still light. There were ribbons of pale blue, and a pink tint that looked burning hot, heaven set on fire.

"Midsummer's Night," Callie said. "When you become who it is you really are."

As they turned into the driveway, the approaching dark was already filling with fireflies. They ran into the house and rummaged around for two glass jars, then returned to the lawn to catch their prey, grabbing in the dark for the blinking globes of light. They brought the jars into the house and drank red wine in a kitchen that was illuminated only by fireflies. They got old books off the shelf, ones that had belonged to Walker when he was a boy. They read Indian stories about turtles that had made islands in the sea, and about a Viking named Thorwald who was said to be buried on a beach nearby, along with the ballast from his ship. They read that whales were thought to have the ability to chart the way home through the centuries, even when the landscape changed, when inlets were filled in and dike roads were built where once there had only been water. For them, the map remained the same.

At midnight, Emma and Callie went back out to the lawn with the fireflies. They set them all free, unscrewing the jars in the meadow, making certain to avoid the poison ivy. Emma spun in a circle, and the light reflected off her skin. If this was the night when a person's deepest self was revealed, then what was inside Emma as she twirled in the field, with the scent of pine and salt in the air? What she wished for most was to be the self she might have been if she'd never been sick, the person she could have become if she hadn't been stopped in some way, if she hadn't stopped herself. She looked at her hands in the firefly light, and she thought her husband had been right all along: she hadn't been there.

The next morning, Emma went down to the general store while Callie slept in. She bought the *Boston Globe* and some pancake mix, and then, at the very last moment, a bucket of white paint. Foolish, really. Total mistake. She'd never use it. She'd never painted a room, let alone a house. Up at the register, she asked Siggy if she knew of a good real-estate agent.

"My cousin, Linda. She'd be only too happy to come look at your house, if that's what you're thinking." Siggy wrote out the phone number. "I called one of the Crosby boys and he'll be by to clean up that shed and the fallen timber. Whether you stay or whether you go, all that wood lying about is a hazard."

Emma made pancake batter when she got back to the house, adding the strawberries that had caused so much trouble. Because Callie was still asleep, she telephoned her mother down in Florida.

"I can't believe you gave me this house. I don't even like houses," Emma said. "I'm a city girl."

"You always liked that one," Katherine told her. "When you first saw it you said it was the most beautiful place, even though it was the edge of the world and we might fall off. You were very brave."

"Remember Siggy Maguire? She said to say hi. She's still picking your blueberries."

"One time I bought groceries there and Siggy ran out after us into the parking lot. She told me you were special."

"Yeah, I was special, all right. I was half bald and skinny as a rail. Remember, my hair grew in black for a while. I was a witch, Mother."

"Siggy didn't mean it like that. She had tears in her eyes."

"I don't know if I'm keeping it," Emma said. "The house."

"It was bought on impulse, so it will probably be sold on impulse," Katherine said. "I wish I was there with you."

"Is there any such thing as turnip jam?" Emma asked before she hung up. "I found a whole bunch of turnips in the field."

"Chutney," her mother suggested. "Try that. That was next on my list, but we never got around to it."

When Callie woke up, her poison-ivy itch was worse than ever. The bumps on her arms were as swollen as bee stings. She had no interest in the strawberry pancakes, and why should she? She'd already decided to go home.

"I'm sorry to do this to you," she told Emma. "I hate to cut our weekend short, but I'm miserable."

They packed up the car, but at the last minute, Emma left her own bags in the hall.

"I'm not going with you. I don't want you to go out of your way for me. It will be faster if you just go directly to New York, and I can easily take the bus. It stops right on the corner by the general store."

"No," Callie said. "I'd feel like a flat-leaver."

"It's no big deal. Plus, I'm going to make turnip chutney. See?" There were the turnips lined up on the countertop. "I've got to stay. And I promise—I'll send you some."

"The crying potion? No thanks. I don't favor turnips."

Emma stood in the driveway and waved. She'd forgotten how still it was here; sometimes the wind was the only thing a person heard. She went out to the field and found twelve more turnips, each one a rosy-brown color, tinged purple and white at the edges. Even forgotten things grew, neatly, it seemed, in a row.

Emma liked the earthy smell as she boiled the turnips in the kitchen, then diced them, along with onion and dried rosemary. The jelly jars were under the sink, and she washed them and boiled them in an old lobster pot. By now the windows of the house were too steamed up to look through. She thought about the person she'd been before she'd been ill, and the person she had become, and she didn't see the slightest similarity. Who was that girl who people ran after in parking lots? Who brought tears to a stranger's eyes? What might she have done if she hadn't woken one morning with a swelling under her arm? Who might she have been able to love?

Emma was thinking about this when she saw something outside the window. She felt a chill then, even though the kitchen was hot. As on any jam-making day, the temperature had risen since Emma had begun. It was always that way. Emma and her mother had made jam in the old fallen-down shed, never here in the kitchen, and now Emma knew why. The room had grown terribly warm. It was almost unbearable. Every window was steamy and damp, and water ran down the glass like teardrops.

Through the steam and the glass, a shadow fell across the floor, a dark blink in the golden daylight. Had Emma seen something outside? She went to the window and cleared a circle of steam with the palm of her hand. There used to be coyotes, she remembered that, and this movement had been darting and quick, the way coyotes were. There used to be blackbirds, and whatever was out there was flickery, just flitting by.

Emma saw nothing when she looked into the yard, but she left the jars boiling and went to have a closer look. There was sure to be no one there, she was all but convinced of it. She went striding out, confident she had imagined the shadow, sure of it really, and so she almost walked right into him: a boy of about ten, with blond hair. Quick as a coyote, clearly. Cautious as a blackbird, certainly. But nervy enough to watch her through the window. Not on his own property, that much was obvious. A little trespasser, it seemed.

"I beg your pardon," Emma said tartly.

"You don't have to." The boy had a matter-of-fact, serious face. "It's your house."

"That's right. I know it's mine. I'm Emma. I used to spend summers here."

She remembered that local people used to joke that the

woods were haunted, that figures slipped in and out of the shadows. Emma's brother, Walker, now consumed with facts and statistics, had believed in such things. *Just because you don't see a ghost*, he once told Emma, *doesn't mean he's not there.*

This boy in Emma's yard had scratches all down his arms from jumping around in the brambles. He'd taken the laces out of his sneakers, and his ankles had a wobbly, coltish look. He was probably a fast runner. He could probably tell you the name of every constellation in the sky.

"What are you making in there?" He was looking past Emma, through the door. Even out here, they could hear the roiling water in the big pot on the stove and the jars clinking as they boiled.

"Turnip chutney. It's like jam."

The boy wrinkled his nose. "Ugh. Turnips are good for nothing."

"You'd be surprised," Emma said. "You didn't say who you were, you know."

"I come here and go fishing all the time," the boy said. "Don't tell anyone or I'll get into trouble."

"From your mother?"

She saw now he had hazel eyes, the kind that could look green or gray or brown depending on his mood. She saw something there she used to feel herself and had forgotten about until this exact moment.

"She's dead," the boy said.

Emma took a step back. "Are you the Crosby boy Siggy sent over to clear out the shed?"

The boy looked at Emma as though he could see her clearly for what she was: a fool who wasn't even grateful to be alive.

"I'm ten," he said. "I don't work. That's my father."

He nodded, and Emma saw there was indeed a truck pulled over in the field, right in the spot where she'd found the turnips. The boy's father was gathering the moldering oak planking, the roof shingles, the nails. The bed of the truck was already filled with wood, old branches, rotten floorboards, good for nothing or good for everything, it was impossible to tell.

"I caught a hundred fireflies last night," Emma said. "I read a book by their light."

"No you didn't." The boy had his hands on his hips. He wanted to believe her, but he didn't know whether or not he should.

"Come inside," Emma told him. "I'll show you how to make turnip chutney. We'll see if it's any good."